MURDER AT THE MESA ROADHOUSE

**by
Jere' Bishop Franco**

Promethean Press

Dallas   Vancouver   Ontario

MURDER AT THE MESA ROADHOUSE

Published by:
Promethean Press
1846 Rosemeade Parkway #192
Carrollton, TX 75007

ISBN 0-9731745-8-7

Manufactured in the United States of America

This book would not have been possible without the invaluable contributions of my technical advisor, James Colon Bishop II. My brother is a highly-decorated military veteran who, after serving over twenty years in the army, worked for several more years in a metropolitan police department and a small-town police department. Now retired, he, for reasons passing understanding, took an interest in my project. Skipper, as he is known to his family, was there to answer questions concerning police officers' routines, gun calibres, and investigative processes. With his help, I created one of the pivotal characters in the book, Officer David De Vargas. Every town in America should have such a cop.

As always, I dedicate my book to my husband, Arturo and my children, Brie, Luke, John and James who make my life worthwhile.

Jere' Bishop Franco

MURDER AT THE MESA ROADHOUSE

La Mesa Noticia, Sunday, June 2

The Town Calendar

The First Baptist Church is sponsoring a Singles Social on Wednesday night at 8 p.m.
Babysitting will be provided.

♦♦♦

The Ladies Garden Club holds meetings on the first Monday of each month at the Mesa Public Library. Randolph Sterling will be installed as President this Monday at 9 a.m.

♦♦♦

As part of World War II Celebration Month, the Blue Eagle Cafe will have a "Fifty-Cent Blue Plate Special" all week. Cost is $3.99.

♦♦♦

St. Francis Church will begin "English As a Second Language" Classes on Tuesday. Residents who wish to learn Spanish are urged to attend.

♦♦♦

(Editor's Note: Yesterday's story on the Normandy invasion should have read "we dedicate this to all those who lived through the long, hot summer of 1944" NOT "we dedicate this to all those who *loved* through the long, hot summer of 1944.)

CHAPTER ONE

"Now don't say anything to anyone until I call my granddaughter," Dorothy O'Daniels said as she turned the sign in the window to "Closed." She waved at the last two customers who were walking to their car.

"So you haven't called her yet?" asked her friend and fellow waitress, Marlene Jankovitch.

"No, I haven't had time. I just learned the news this morning. You're the first to know. And it's too late now. I'll call her tomorrow. Or later today," she laughed since the clock over the door told her that it was already 2:30 in the morning.

While speaking, Dorothy deftly emptied the cash register, counted the currency twice, and placed the contents in the time-lock safe located beneath the counter. She registered the amount in the ledger.

"Did you think to . . . ?" Marlene made a gesture with her hand.

"No, I plum forgot. I'll do that when I get home."

"Well, I got to be going. I'm taking the early shift tomorrow," said Marlene.

"You don't need a ride? George is coming for me. We can take you home."

"No, I got somebody waiting."

"You go ahead. I'll lock up." Dorothy turned back to the ledger.

Marlene walked through the kitchen and waved at Hector, the cook, who was scrubbing his stove. "See you in the morning, Hector.

"Night, Marlene. Dorothy, you going to be okay?"

"Yeah, Hector. I just want to tally these tickets one more time. They just don't come out right."

"Lock up behind me," he cautioned as he also exited through the back door.

Dorothy, who had been closing the restaurant for the last forty years, dutifully locked the door behind the young Hispanic man, turned off the kitchen lights and then returned to the large calculator and pile of tickets. After several minutes, she found her mistake and redid the ledger.

Must be all the excitement, she thought with a thrill of pleasure. She placed the tickets and ledger in a cloth pouch which she put under the counter. Then she reached for her purse.

"Is someone there?" she asked cautiously as she sensed a presence standing in the doorway to the kitchen. "What are you - ?"

Dorothy never finished the sentence. The bullet, which was shot from close range, hit vital arteries in her heart, and she slumped to the floor in a silent heap.

Thirty minutes later Patrolman David De Vargas exited the Interstate and pulled into the parking lot of the Mesa Roadhouse. As the newest member of the police department, he always worked the midnight shift from 11 p.m. to 7 a.m. Every night he drove by the restaurant as part of his routine.

It's awfully late for anyone to still be working, he thought as he noted the light over the counter. Usually all the lights except for the outdoor lamp were turned off when all the employees had left. Rapping on the restaurant door, he received no response. Because there were no lights other than the dim lamp behind the cash register, he could detect no movement. He decided to try the back door which he discovered to be unlocked. Pulling his revolver, he stepped carefully into the kitchen and moved slowly toward the counter where he had sat countless times drinking coffee. His worst fears were realized when he saw Dorothy O'Daniels lying on the floor. Kneeling down, he felt for a pulse which he didn't really expect to find. Too much blood.

Straightening up, David took a deep breath. Having been born and raised in Mesa, he had known Dorothy O'Daniels his entire life. He could remember her advising him to enlist in the army when he graduated from high school and was unsure of his future. She had also been the one to encourage him to attend Mesa State University after his four-year military stint. After receiving a degree in Criminal Justice, he had joined the force last year. She had marked the event by baking him one of her famous carrot cakes.

David reached into his side pocket and pulled out his walkie-talkie.

"Helen, we'll need Gary over here at the Mesa Roadhouse with his camera and fingerprint kit. And an ambulance."

"Sure honey," said the plump, middle-aged woman who had known him since kindergarten. David knew that she also played bingo weekly with Dorothy and Marlene.

"And tell Chief Cummings to get over here right away. Wake

4

him up if you have to."

"What's happened David?"

"Dorothy O'Daniels is dead," he said grimly. Over the phone, he could hear the woman weeping.

That would be the response of the entire town, he thought.

Shea took one last look around the apartment. The moving company had already packed the things they were transporting, mostly boxes of books, some camping gear, and their much used computer equipment. She had hovered nearby while the men carefully loaded the music system which included an old-fashioned turntable for records and the combination color television-VCR on which she and her husband had watched countless videos when they couldn't afford dinner and a movie. After some hesitation, she had also allowed them to pack her husband's most prized possession, a Bushnell telescope. The only furniture they had acquired in their five years of marriage had been an inexpensive computer desk and swivel chair, purchased at one of the many second-hand furniture stores which lined University Avenue. These also went into the moving van. Because Joe had told her she wouldn't need any linens, dishes, or kitchen appliances, she had sold those things in an apartment sale and raised a couple of hundred dollars. She had also sold most of Mark's physics texts and clothes although she gave a few of his books away to friends at their request. Since her financial condition was far from rosy, she would need that money in the months to come.

After putting her suitcase and garment bag into the small ten-year-old Honda, Shea went back to the second floor apartment for her backpack and to look around the apartment one last time.

I was happy here, Shea thought, picking up a pewter frame with a photograph of a young Asian man wearing a University of Arizona sweatshirt and black-framed glasses.

He looked far younger than his twenty-eight years, too young to be a Ph.D. candidate in physics. She put the photograph in her backpack. From the refrigerator she took out the one remaining item, a red rose wrapped in green tissue paper.

A knock at her open door caused her to look around and smile. Her best friend stood in the doorway with two paper bags.

"MacDonald's orange juice and Egg McMuffins," she announced as she breezed into the living room which was spotless and denude of any sign of residency.

5

"Hi, Jerri."

"You know it's really unfair. You don't look pregnant at all unless you turn sideways," said Jerri. As usual, she looked stunning. Short, blonde, and dimpled, she turned heads wherever she went.

"Well, I am, seven months and counting," said Shea.

"Are you going to be okay on this trip? It's what, twelve hours?"

"Not quite. I'll be okay. If I get tired, I'll stay overnight in El Paso. I love the food there," said Shea.

"Have you heard anything from any of the universities?"

Shea shook her head. "You know Mark and I had decided that I should take a year off to have the baby. And then when everything went wrong, I began to apply. But I just keep getting these rejection letters saying that the positions are all filled."

"I know it's hard, especially since you're expecting. You were the most pregnant
Ph.D. at the graduation," joked Jerri.

Shea laughed. Jerri could always perk up any day or any situation. Here she was a pregnant, out-of-work single mom, but at least she had completed her dream and earned a doctoral degree in American History.

"It's good that you have someone you can go to for help," Jerri was saying.

"I know. Joe has been great. And she doesn't really have to do this," said Shea with feeling.

Unwillingly her mind turned to her mother and sister. Five years ago, when she had graduated from the University of Dallas, she had been offered scholarships for graduate work at the University of New Mexico and the University of Arizona. Her mother had strongly objected to Shea leaving Dallas, because Shea's older sister, Megan, had just divorced and moved back into their tiny apartment during the previous year with her four-year-old daughter, Shannon.

"I need you to help with the bills and with babysitting," her mother argued.

Shea had remained adamant. She knew that if she stayed she would never get out of a vicious cycle which had been a problem for years. Her mother was obsessed with Megan's daughter, Shannon, and would do anything to have them around. Anything often meant that Shea spent a great deal of time babysitting and keeping house while her mother accompanied Megan on fruitless interviews for modeling jobs. Although she was a beautiful girl, the agencies invariably told her that she was too short to model.

Undeterred Megan continued to work in the cosmetics department at the department store where her mother was a billing clerk, to date frequently, and to hope for a big break.

"Are you thinking about your mother?" asked Jerri when Shea became too quiet.

"Yeah, sometimes I still feel guilty for walking out on her."

"Guilt is something that Jewish people invented and hold first place among all people for the trait. Although you Catholics certainly come in a close second." She swallowed a bite of sweet roll and continued. "Stop feeling that way. You had a right to your own life. Is she still not speaking to you?"

"It's on again, off again. She always becomes very angry whenever I visit Joe. And when I told her last month that Joe had invited me to stay for as long as I needed, she hung up."

"She'll get over it. My mom always does," said Jerri nonchalantly.

Shea admired the way that Jerri could deal with her own mother's manipulations and games. As a matter of fact, she admired a great deal about Jerri.

"Good advice," she said. "Now remember that you have promised to visit. Especially when the baby is born."

"Will do. By then I will really be flush with cash," said Jerri. "And we'll do the town red. Whatever there is to do in that little town."

"Great. I've got to get going," said Shea reluctantly.

She could have stayed forever in Tucson, the town where she had fallen in love, married, and been happy for possibly the first time in her life. Happy and secure. At least for a while Mark had given her that.

"Good luck with your new job," she told her friend.

Jerri, who looked like a runaway teenager most of the time and was constantly carded whenever she and Shea went to a nightclub, had just passed her bar exam and landed a job with the district attorney's office. She was deceptively sweet-looking, incredibly beautiful, and probably had more men hitting on her than Pamela Lee Anderson, thought Shea. She was also brilliant.

They hugged one last time, and then Shea, after stopping by the manager's office to turn in her key, headed down Park Avenue. It was already seven o'clock in the morning, and she wanted to get as many miles behind her as she could before the unrelenting southwestern sun began its afternoon baking session. There was just one last stop that she had to make. At Lancaster Avenue she turned right and then left again into a well-kept, grassy park. She drove slowly through the lanes until she came to her chosen location and parked. From the front seat of her car, she picked up the rose. Afterwalking several feet, she stopped in front of a white marble headstone, kneeled down and placed the rose on the grave.

"Mark, why did you have to step in front of that car?" she murmured. "Why did you have to leave me?"

At eight o'clock that evening, Officer David De Vargas sat in the kitchen of Dorothy O'Daniels home, drinking coffee with her gardener and handyman who lived rent-free in the apartment over the garage. He had already questioned everyone at the restaurant who had left some time before Dorothy was murdered. He was now making his way through all her friends and acquaintances, taking statements and hearing a variety of scenarios concerning her murder.

"I think it was one of those homeless hobos who are always passing through town," George said. "You know, one of them transients." He pronounced the word as "tran-zent."

"You might be right. Did Dorothy have any arguments with anyone lately?"

"No, none that I kin think of. Ever'body liked Dorothy. She'd give ya the shirt off her back."

"That's true," agreed David.

Most people to whom he had spoken that day favored the transient robber theory. In other words, a transient happened to come by the restaurant when Dorothy was alone hoping to find some money in the cash register. When he was disappointed to find nothing in the machine, he shot Dorothy and took her purse.

That might work except that he doubted that a transient would take the whole purse. The wallet, yes. He could stick that in his pocket and walk away without anyone noticing. If the murderer was a hobo, David suspected he was hitchhiking since few homeless people who passed through Mesa had cars. He couldn't very well walk around carrying a woman's purse. And they had yet to find the handbag in the immediate vicinity.

Unless it was a female transient. That thought had popped into David's mind several times. As a matter of fact, he wasn't entirely convinced of the transient theory which is why he had called Chief Beau Cummings the next afternoon to ask if he could do a little investigating on his own.

"Sure thing, son," said the Chief who had also known David since he was born. As a matter of fact, he had been partner to David's father when he had been on the police force. "Just don't get in Aaron's way. You know how he likes to do things in a particular order. He doesn't like to be second-guessed."

Aaron Kominski was the department investigator. Tall, slender and fortyish, he was always impeccably dressed in suit and tie. He had been hired specifically by the mayor from a Fort Worth police department at a higher salary than was usual for small-town investigators. The mayor had insisted that he was worth every penny, because of his excellent record in resolving criminal cases. One had to overlook, he argued, some small personality quirks.

David wasn't so sure. First, there weren't many murders in a small town like Mesa. Dorothy O'Daniels' death had shaken up the entire population who had learned about the murder before most of them had their second cup of morning coffee. Second, he thought that Kominski had too many preconceptions about small-town life in West Texas as well as a few prejudices to boot. He patronized the locals as if he considered them brainless hicks who had been given lobotomies at birth. And those were the Anglo people. The Mexican residents, both those born in Mexico and those born on the American side, he treated with ill-concealed contempt and made no attempt to learn the language or any of the social customs of the area.

His attitude toward David was simple. David was invisible and didn't exist. When he had turned in his initial report to the sergeant during the second shift, Kominski had barely looked at it.

"Looks open and closed to me," he said to Assistant Chief Jaime Chavez as he dropped the report on his desk without a glance in David's direction. "Probably a transient. Happens all the time. These old dames shouldn't be working so late anyway. They're taking a huge risk."

His off-hand dismissal of Dorothy O'Daniels' death galled David, and he would have spoken, but Lopez gave him a stern look. Lopez, ten years his senior, was the department ambassador, a skilled negotiator at soothing ruffled feathers and keeping tempers cooled.

"I'm sure you will pursue all leads," he said in a noncommital tone to Kominski.

"Yeah, I think I will begin by interviewing that wetback cook." Ignoring the sour look that passed between David and Jaime, Kominski got up and left the room.

"I know you're upset, David, because you knew her so well and

9

really liked her. We all did. Just don't but heads with Kominski. You'll regret it," advised Lopez.

"Why don't you tell the Chief whatever it is that you're thinking of doing."

That was why David was now sitting in Dorothy's kitchen with George Fallchurch. He had called the Chief at home who had given him the green light to ask questions of relatives and friends, but only after Kominski had interviewed them. David hadn't slept since he found Dorothy, and he was on duty again tonight until seven in the morning. He poured himself a second cup of coffee just as the telephone rang. George picked up the wall telephone next to the refrigerator.

"O'Daniels house," he said bluntly as if he could summon up the mistress of the house at will. "No, she's not here. Oh, is that you kiddo? I got some very bad news. Your grandmother is dead. Are you still there? Did you hear me?"

David glanced up, his body tense and alert. He knew who was on the other end of the telephone, and he didn't envy George's task in relating this information. He looked down at his coffee cup and without effort envisioned the lovely face of the young woman he had not seen for years. Despite several relationships, including one short-lived engagement, he had never gotten over his crush on her. The first time he saw her, at the age of fifteen, she was a twelve-year-old girl who was eating an ice cream cone and watching George trim the hedge. Her dark brown hair was cut in a chin-length bob and her dark grey eyes watched carefully as George explained how to use the shears. She never turned around to see him staring.

Over the years she visited her grandmother infrequently, but he always knew when she was in town. He had watched her change from a shy, introverted teenager into a warm and confident young woman. Despite the fact that many young women found him attractive, he had never managed to get her attention. He serious-ly doubted that she even knew he existed.

"Okay, kiddo, please stop crying," George was saying after lis-tening intently for a few moments. "Everything's going to be all right. Jason Tyler is taking care of all the arrangements." He paused again. "Okay I'll see you soon."

"God, she must be devastated. She was so devoted to her grandmother," said David with sincere sympathy. He added in as casual a tone as he could manage, "Is she coming?"

George looked at him shrewdly. David's attempt at innocence didn't fool him.

"She's had a rough time so don't you go trying anything, boy."

"No, sir, I won't," David promised. He wondered how long he could keep that promise.

From her Holiday Inn room, Shea could see both the Rio Grande River and El Cristo Del Rey. The thirty foot statue of Christ the King, built by a visionary priest and a small, poor but dedicated parish in the 1930s, stood in solitary glory on a small mountain peak which separated Ciudad Juarez, Mexico from El Paso, Texas. On one of their long road trips, she and Mark had climbed the mountain trail to the top where visitors could view the two countries and two states, both Texas and New Mexico. Legends concerning the statue bounded in local folklore. One of the most famous stories involved a young boy who went to the statue to pray for his mother to recover from an illness. He stumbled and was in danger of falling off the mountain. Miraculously he was saved when the statue stretched out his hand and grabbed the boy's arm.

At this moment, Shea felt like she was falling, and there was no one to reach out and catch her. Putting her face in her hands, she wept silently and deeply. Her beloved Grandmother Joe, as she had always called Dorothy Josephine O'Daniels, was dead, murdered. After a while, she stopped crying and decided that she should tell her relatives in Dallas. Because she was unsure if they would accept a collect call, she used a pre-paid calling card. When noone answered at her mother's apartment, she called her Aunt Shirley.

"She's in Las Vegas with Megan," said Aunt Shirley. "They made up again. Megan had been living with her boyfriend, but they broke up. She moved back in with your mother, and they decided to take a trip to the casinos. You know how much they love going there. Shannon is staying with friends."

"Do you know what hotel she's staying in?" asked Shea wearily. This was usual with her mother. She went on trips, moved in and out of apartments, and changed jobs, all without notifying her youngest daughter. Shea sometimes had to call several relatives before finding her newest address.

"No, I don't, but I'll tell her the news when she gets back which should be tomorrow or the day after that. I'm so sorry. And I'm sorry about your husband, too. We just couldn't make it to the funeral, honey, I had such migraine headaches so bad that week you just can't imagine. . ."

Shea listened while her aunt repeated a litany of complaints which she usually did whenever Shea called. She loved her aunt, who was funny and loving, but tonight Shea could barely pay attention. After hanging up, she lay on her bed, too exhausted to go out for dinner. If Mark had been there with her, they would have gone to Casa Jurado for enchiladas. If Grandmother Joe had been there they would have driven to Chico's Tacos on the other side of town. Chico's was a small, fast-food place, but they made the best rolled tacos in the city.

Now both people whom she loved more than anything in the world were gone. Tomorrow she would drive to Mesa, Texas where she would soon see her grandmother buried. After that, she didn't know what she would do. The thought of returning to her family in Dallas was unbearable. She feared she would never have her independence or her own life. Perhaps in Mesa she could find some part-time teaching jobs at the community college or the local university while she continued to apply elsewhere for tenure-track positions.

At least she didn't have any outstanding debts, thought Shea as she lay on the bed mentally making budget calculations. Because Mark was always offered lucrative summer internships at NASA and Texas Instruments, they were able to avoid incurring any student loans. Both of them worked as teaching or research assistants during the fall and spring terms which paid their monthly rent. The Honda, antique though it was, was at least paid for and cheap to run. Finally, the student benefits which were available to all teaching assistants had paid for Mark's burial and Shea's prenatal care. Before she left the university she had checked with human resources. Her health care premiums were covered by the University until August, whether she was in Arizona or Texas. After that, as an alumni, she had the option of purchasing inexpensive monthly premiums.

Shea had closed her bank account in Tucson and withdrawn the last of her money, $2,431. Sleepily she wondered how long that would last. Car insurance, health insurance, rent, food, diapers, formula. Making lists of monthly expenses in her head ultimately served the same purpose as counting sheep. Before she was aware, she had drifted off to sleep.

"I didn't know that you would be here, Berta," said Marlene Jankovitch, walking into the bedroom where the woman was shifting through the closet. Berta Rivera, who was on hr hands and knees, jumped up with a start.

"Ay Dios mio," exclaimed the heavyset maid, placing a hand on her heart. "I didn't hear you come in, Miss Duffy. It's those rubber-soled shoes you always wear."

"What are you doing?" asked Marlene, patting Berta sympa-thetically on the shoulder.

"I'm looking for something for Miss O'Daniels to wear for the Visitation and the Funeral. Mr. Tyler asked me to help." Despite the fact that she had cleaned house for Dorothy O'Daniels for twenty years and that Dorothy had always asked her to call her by her Christian name, Berta had never dropped the "miss" title.

"I can do that for you. Why don't you go downstairs and fix something for Shea?
She'll be getting in soon won't she?"

"Yes, ma'm, and I can't wait to see her. She called on her cell phone and said she would be here by lunchtime."

"That's good. Well, you go on now, and I'll do this for you."

"Thank you ma'm," said Berta, grateful to be relinquishing the task. It had made her even sadder to look at the beautiful suits that Miss O'Daniels would never wear again, and she was happy to hand over the responsibility to that nice lady who had worked with her at the restaurant. In the large old-fashioned kitchen, which had thankfully been remodeled since the house was first built in 1899, she checked on the sopaipilla and beans simmering on the mod-ern gas range.

Miss O'Daniels always had modern appliances and old-fash-ioned furniture, she thought to herself. She then removed a tray of cheese enchiladas from the oven which she knew were favorites of Dorothy's granddaughter. They were favorites of that cute hus-band of hers also, she recalled with another flood of feelings. So heartbreaking, she told herself with a sigh, to lose your abuelita and esposo in the same year.

"I think that's her car comin' down the road now," said George who had entered the dining room where Berta was setting the mahogany Georgian table with Wedgwood china and Gorsham sil-ver. "That's kind of fancy for lunch, ain't it?"

"We have to cheer her up, so don't you say anything," said Berta fiercely.
Although she was fond of George, she never stood on ceremony with him.

"Just askin'," he grumbled and went outside to stand on the front porch. "Here she comes."

Moments later, a beaming George was carrying in suitcases. In the foyer Shea dropped her backpack to throw her arms around Berta.

"Com' estas, mi hija?"

"Muy bien, gracias. Y usted senora?" Shea replied formally.

"Tu eres muy flaca. No estas comiendo?"

"I'm eating fine," lied Shea. She spoke in English for George's sake. No matter that he had been born in the area, he had never learned Spanish and not from a lack of trying. He just couldn't wrap his tongue around it, he often said. "What's for lunch?"

"Tu favorita. Enchiladas, frijoles, sopaipilla," said Berta as she bustled off to get ice tea from the refrigerator.

"Why are there four plates? Is someone else coming?"

"Marlene is upstairs," said George. "She'll want to stuff her face with Berta's cooking."

"Marlene from the restaurant?" asked Shea. "Was she there when grandmother was . . ."

She couldn't finish the sentence. She just couldn't say the words.

"No, she had already left when it happened. Thank God, or there would be two of them." Realizing that she sounded unfeeling, Berta added hurriedly, "I'll go get her."

"No, I'll go. Where is she?"

"She's looking through your grandmother's clothes for something she can be buried in."

Upstairs Shea knocked softly on her grandmother's bedroom door so that she wouldn't catch Marlene by surprise. She was afraid the woman, who had worked with her grandmother for six years, might be sitting up here alone and crying.

"Oh my God," exclaimed Marlene. She closed a drawer in the marble-topped maple dresser, an antique like most of the furniture in the house. Several outfits were thrown on top of the Battenburg lace bedspread covering the matching bed. Shea knew that the bedroom suite originally belonged to her great-great-grandmother for whom the house was built. Marlene came over and hugged Shea, then held her at arm's length.

"You look tired sweetie," Marlene said soothingly. Shea smiled. She couldn't help but be comforted by all the mothering she was receiving. It had always been that way in her grandmother's home.

"I'm fine. It was just such a long drive. And then to have this happen." Shea's voice broke and the tears she had held back now flowed. "Who could have done this, Marlene?"

"Probably some poor schmuck who thought the restaurant was

14

deserted, and then discovered Dorothy there. I think she was just in the way of a simple robbery."

"Somehow that makes it worse," said Shea. "It makes her death senseless, meaningless."

"No, no it don't. Nobody had a better life than your grandma. She was the best friend I ever had. They'll find the guy who did this."

Shea looked again at all the clutter in the room. Jewels and scarves littered the dresser, hats were thrown into chairs, and shoes lay scattered on the floor.

"I wanted just the right things for her. You know how picky she was about her

looks," explained Marlene. "I hope you don't mind."

Shea shook her head. "Of course not."

Her grandmother never missed her weekly hair appointment, and she loved to shop for clothes. At seventy-four, she was trim, vital, and still turned heads even though her own had turned grey.

"Why don't we finish this after lunch?" Marlene put her arm around Shea's shoulder and led her downstairs.

It took only a little coaxing to convince Berta to join them. During lunch, Berta, Marlene and George filled Shea in on the latest gossip, including recent marriages, births, and newly elected councilmen. Everyone seemed determined to avoid the subject of the murder.

"Well, kids, I got to get going. We're training a new cook, and she don't know how to use the ice machine. I'll come by tomorrow, Shea, and we'll take something over to MacKenzie's Funeral Home. If you want I can go through Dorothy's things and take them away to donate to the church or Goodwill. I think that's what she would want."

"Let's wait awhile for that," said Shea. The very thought depressed her.

As she helped Berta clear the table, Shea turned to George. "Who found my grandmother?"

"David De Vargas. He's the newest officer on the force."

"That name sounds familiar. Do you think he could come over so I could ask him some questions?"

"I just bet he could be convinced," snorted George. "I'll give him a call."

Mystified at his tone, Shea stared. What was eating George?

❖

That evening David De Vargas walked up the steps to the porch of the white frame Victorian house. He had finally gotten some sleep, but he had dreamed about the murder. In the dream, someone was holding a gun and standing over Dorothy's body. He waited for the person to turn around. Then the dream ended.

George had told him to just enter the foyer when he arrived. As he stood in the hallway, he glanced into the living room on the right. It was furnished in masculine fashion with dark brown leather sofa and club chairs and an eight-foot long dark pine entertainment center. He had heard that Patrick O'Daniels liked to watch football games and drink Irish whiskey in here before he died twenty-five years ago. He suspected that Dorothy O'Daniels did the same. Peering into the parlor on the left, he noted the classic ivory sofa and wing chair, probably covered in real linen. Cherrywood Queen Anne tables and paisley-covered Bergere chairs were grouped in corners along with a burnished oak console piano, which looked like and probably was an authentic antique like everything else in the house. Both front rooms boasted large window seats which gave excellent views of the long, tree-lined circular driveway.

I'm sure I'm the only officer in the whole county who knows the name of this furniture, thought David wryly. His fashion expertise resulted from a two-year relationship with an aspiring interior decorator. Last thing he had heard about her she was living with a doctor in Albuquerque.

"Hello, Officer," said Shea. She had wandered into the foyer from the back kitchen. "Would you mind sitting on the front porch? It's been so long since I've been here, and I just want to feel the fresh air."

He followed her to the veranda and settled his six foot three inch limbs into a white wicker chair with a comfortable blue-striped cushion. Shea chose to perch on the wooden railing and sat dangling one sandal-clad foot while she looked at the sun disappearing behind the pine trees which dominated their town.

David was having trouble not staring at her. He had often heard that pregnant women glowed, but he had never believed it until now. Her fair skin looked translucent, and her eyes were darker than he remembered. She was wearing a denim cotton shirt and white cotton pants. He noted that her only jewelry were small gold earrings, a gold cross necklace, and her wedding band. How long did widows wear their rings? he wondered.

"Would you like some lemonade or tea, officer?"
"That would be fine, ma'm. And my name is David. David De Vargas."

She had disappeared into the house but returned in seconds with a silver tray and two crystal goblets, one of which she handed to him with a smile. "Weren't you in the military before you went to the police academy?"

"Yes. I served a four-year tour."

"I remember my grandmother talking about you. You were quite a hero here in the town. Didn't you rescue some people over in Bosnia? Earn some medals?"

He cleared his throat. "That was a long time ago."

"I'm sorry. I didn't mean to get personal."

She looked so chastened that he regretted his sharpness. "It's just that, what I did, well it was our job. I don't know that I should have gotten any medals."

"I understand," she said. "What can you tell me about my grandmother's
murder?"

"We're checking all leads, ma'm. Sergeant Kominski has interviewed everyone who worked at the restaurant that night and most of the people who went there for a meal. Nobody remembers seeing anyone suspicious hanging around."

"What about evidence? Can you tell me about that?"

"There are a lot of fingerprints at the restaurant of course. It's impossible to say for sure, but we haven't found any unusual prints. People have cooperated about giving fingerprint samples. Whoever did this either wore gloves or didn't touch the cash register before he killed Dorothy."

"What about the gun?"

"It was a Smith and Wesson Chief, a five-shot revolver which used 38 special bullets. Not a highly unusual gun. Lots of people, men and women, around here carry them."

"Can't you get a list of whoever has one of those?"

David nodded in sympathy. People were usually anxious to find a simple solution to a murder investigation. And when that person was a relative, it was even more frustrating to encounter roadblocks.

"We've done that already, ma'm. We've questioned everyone who lives in the vicinity, and there are about twenty of them, who owned one of these guns. So far every pistol is accounted for, and the owners showed no signs of gunshot residue. In fact, each of them had a perfectly good alibi for the morning of the murder. Of course, there are always a few people who have unregistered guns. There's no way of tracking those."

"Would it be probable that a transient would have one of those guns?"

David was hoping she wouldn't think along those lines. It would mean that there was an armed robber out there who had already murdered for a little cash and might do so again.

"Yes, ma'm. It's always possible. We've passed this information along to other police stations in all directions to watch for anyone behaving in a suspicious manner. If this was a transient, he'll do this again and hopefully be caught."

"Well, thanks Officer for your time. I know that you have a lot of rounds to make, and I need to get some rest."

"Yes, ma'm." He walked to the steps to leave and then turned around. "Mrs. Chan, there is one thing."

"Sure." Shea paused in the doorway.
"Well, that ring that Dorothy was wearing. It's pretty expensive, isn't it?"

"Yes, as a matter of fact, it is. My grandfather bought it for her on their twentieth wedding anniversary. It's platinum with five diamond carats." As she was describing the ring, Shea looked at the young officer with a dawning realization. In the envelope which held Dorothy's personal things and which had been returned to her earlier, Shea had found her grandmother's gold Cartier watch and the diamond ring. If the robber was looking for money or valuables, why hadn't he stolen the jewelry?

Shea's Enchiladas

8 corn tortillas
2 tb corn oil
8 oz shredded cheese
1/4 cup onions

1 package red chile sauce
1 can tomato sauce
1 small can olives,
diced

1. Mix chile and tomato sauce together. Fry tortillas until soft. Arrange in tray.
2. Mix cheese, onions, olives. Spoon 1/8 mixture into each tortilla.
3. Fold over tortillas, fasten with toothpick.
4. Bake at 350 degrees for 15-20 minutes.

Spanish/English Translation

Ay Dios mio. Oh, my God.

Com' estas mi hija. How are you, my daughter?

Muy bien gracias. Y usted senora? Very well, thank you. And you ma'm?

Tu eres muy flaca. No estas comiendo? You are very skinny. Aren't you eating?

Tu favorita. Enchiladas, frijoles, sopaipilla. Your favorite. Enchiladas, beans, rice.

Editorial

Until 1875 Mesa, Texas was not much more than a dusty out-post in the west Texas desert. Composed of St. Francis Church, which also provided education for the area's children, a general store, which also functioned as a post office, and a dozen farmers, including a few which retained their original land grants from the King of Spain, the settlement might have been absorbed into a larger town site had it not been for the Southern Pacific Railroad. In 1875 the railroad sent Angus O'Daniels, an engineer, to oversee the construction of the railroad lines which would be a part of the extensive infrastructure connecting the entire southwest.

In 1880 O'Daniels and two other prominent town residents, Ignacio De Vargas, a descendent of an original Tejano settler, and James Svenson, owner of Svenson's Mercantile, lobbied the Texas Legislature for incorporation as a town. In June, 1882 the legislature granted Mesa a city charter.

Next summer marks the 1,120th anniversary of Mesa, Teas. We should start planning the festivities now. Get on a committee, write your city council representative, take an active part!

(Editor's Note: Sunday's mention of bilingual classes should have read "Residents who wish to learn English are urged to attend.)

CHAPTER TWO

During the next two days, Shea had little time to mull over possible murder theories. She was too busy preparing for the funeral. On Tuesday she drove her Honda downtown to do the necessary errands in person. At St. Francis Church, a beautiful church built in the southwestern Mission style and located only a block from the town plaza, she consulted Father Rinconi about the Rosary and funeral Mass.

"For the Rosary we could use the church choir and organist. They do some beautiful Handel numbers. I think you should use the church folk group for the funeral, because Dorothy usually attended the service when they performed. They do more contemporary things, including quite a few songs from "Godspell.""

"Joe loved music of all kinds," recalled Shea. "She would even listen to classical with me."

"She was a good parishioner. She never missed Sunday Mass," the priest commented. A young, good-looking pastor, he had been with the Parish only five years. Parishioners often saw him jogging early in the morning or playing basketball with high school kids in the afternoon. Everyone called him Father Jim. "There will be a big turnout for the ceremony. Will you be burying her in Shady Grove?"

Shea nodded. "That's where my grandfather was buried. She has a plot right next to him. Did you know that she used to visit his grave at least once a week? I swear she communicated with him somehow."

"That kind of devotion is rare these days. Your grandmother never remarried?"

"No, although she was often asked. She preferred to spend time with her
grandchildren and her friends."

"Will your sister or any other relatives be coming?" Father Jim tried to sound neutral and diplomatic.

"No, my mother finally called and said that Shannon, my niece, had come down with a cold, and she didn't think it was a good idea to travel with her. My grandmother had two older brothers. One of them died of cancer a few years ago. He never married. The other one moved to Australia to raise his family. His children, who are grown now, have called and promised to send flowers. They are also unable to come."

"So you will be representing the family?"

"Yes," said Shea and tried not to sigh. Why did it feel that she had no family left?

"Is there someone to help you in the house?"

"Berta and Marlene have been by every day. Marlene brings soup or sandwiches from the restaurant, and Berta comes to clean up, even though I keep telling her that I can't pay her anything. I was left very short of cash after my husband died. And of course, there's George. He checks the house every night."

Shea didn't mention that she often saw a police cruiser passing by the house. She wasn't sure, but she thought it was David De Vargas.

After finalizing details with the priest, Shea stopped by Edna's Boutique.

Although a new outfit was a luxury she could ill afford, she had to buy something appropriate for the funeral. Since it was already warm in the west Texas town, Edna convinced her to forgo black for navy.

"This is a cute little suit, honey," said Edna Grunderson, the sixty-two-year-old shopkeeper with silver blonde hair. She held up a navy pin-striped maternity vest and knee-length skirt. "You could wear this with that white blouse you have on right now. And if you wear this little hat, it will just make the outfit."

Shea tried on the navy reefer with a short veil and looked in the mirror over the countertop. Somehow the hat added a touch of dignity.

"I'll take it," she said and added, "You might as well throw in the shoes and purse to match." She felt that if she were going to throw caution to the winds, she might as well enjoy it.

"We also have a darling little baby boutique in that next room when you're ready to shop for the little one. It's doing real nice. I'm also going to open a bridal department next door as soon as I can work out a contract with the owner. Their candle shop's going out of business. I told myself, it's just a shame that some of these girls in town go all the way to Midland or El Paso for their wedding gowns. I'd like to get a piece of that business."

Edna chatted without pause as she rang up Shea's purchases.

At age sixty-two, the woman was just as energetic, ambitious and optimistic as she had been at twenty-two. She was also one of the town's most gifted gossipers, and Shea knew well not to say anything she didn't want repeated.

"You know I was so sorry about your grandmother. I've known her for so long even though she was older than me and went to the Catholic Church. I go to First Baptist, you know. How's everything going with the investigation?"

"As well as can be expected," Shea said evasively and escaped from the store.

Her next stop was with William MacKenzie, the funeral director. After viewing several models, Shea chose an oaken casket with lace-trimmed linen lining. It seemed to be the most feminine casket, and she thought it would provide a becoming background for her grandmother's lilac suit on which she and Marlene had finally decided. They discussed visitation hours, music selections, and guest registry books for the Visitation. Finally, Shea spent some time poring over a catalogue and choosing a headstone for the grave.

"How is your daughter?" Shea asked.

She recalled the times that she had seen Vanessa MacKenzie, who was about five years older than herself and incredibly beautiful. In her senior year at college she had been named Mesa State University Homecoming Queen. Vanessa had also won several beauty contests, including Miss West Texas and Miss Black Texas.

William MacKenzie wiped his gold-rimmed glasses with a maroon silk
handkerchief which he then put carefully back into the pocket of his grey pin-striped suit.

"She's doing very well. As a matter of fact, she has finished her residency at Parkland Hospital in Dallas and has come here to work at the clinic. In pediatrics."

"She's a pediatrician? I knew that she was going to medical school, but I didn't know her field."

"Yes, um," he said trying not to sound indelicate. "If you haven't chosen a doctor for your baby yet, I'm sure she would, um, love to have your child as a patient."

"Absolutely," said Shea sincerely. "I will call her immediately."

It was late afternoon before Shea was able to make it to Jason Tyler's office.

"Jason Tyler, Esquire" resided in a glass-fronted office nestled between the "*La Mesa Noticia*" and "Freidrich's Real Estate." All three businesses were located across from the town plaza. As a contemporary of both her grandparents, Jason had been the most affected by her grandmother's death. He called Shea at least three times a day on matters ranging from the terms of the burial policy to the payment of property taxes, which he insisted he would handle from the office.

"Mr. Tyler, thank you so much for everything," Shea said as she sank into a butterscotch leather armchair in his office and accepted a glass of iced tea from Alice Tyler, his secretary and niece.

"Have you made all the funeral arrangements to your satisfaction?" he asked with his usual genteel courtesy.

"Yes, I think everything has been taken care of," she said and recounted her activities for the day. He sat listening with interest and occasionally nodding.

"Have you thought about the reception after the graveside ceremony? You do know there is some money set aside for that?"

"Yes. Berta has agreed to help. She'll cook a few dishes and clean up afterwards. I've called Alberto's Bakery for a cake and some cookies. And I thought you might suggest what would be appropriate to drink."

"I think a nice Chablis, some coffee and iced tea will be sufficient for the guests. Then after everyone has left, we can have the traditional brandy for the Reading of the
Will. I believe Dorothy had some Christian Brothers in the liquor cabinet. If not, the University Beverage Store will have carry it. It was her favorite brand."

"The Reading of the Will?" asked Shea in perplexion. "What is this?"

"Didn't Dorothy tell you? She had a will made years ago. I'm not at liberty to tell you anything about it until everyone is here. But I will tell you this much, Shea. She meant to change the will, considering what has happened to you in the past few months. Unfortunately she died before she could do that."

Shea felt a sinking feeling in her stomach. She had hoped that at the very least she and her baby would have a place to stay until she could find a good position. Now it seemed that even that safe haven was in jeopardy. Perhaps her grandmother had willed her property to the county for a museum. It was certainly her right.

"Who will be at this reading?"

"George Fallchurch, who you know was a very dear friend of both your grandfather and your grandmother. Also Berta Rivera and Marlene Jankovitch. These people will receive certain bequests. The bulk of the estate, however, has been left to you and your sister."

"My mother and sister have already decided not to attend the funeral," said Shea with not a small amount of disgust.

"Oh, they will be there," said Jason with certainty. "I've already spoken to them."

❖

As Shea sat chatting in the solicitor's office, David De Vargas was driving toward the edge of town where the trailer park was located. Officially he was not on duty for another hour, but he had just received a telephone call at his efficiency apartment in "The Cedars" from an old man who said he was calling from a corner store. Notifying Aaron Kominski at the department, David said he would meet him at the address given by the old man who spoke in Spanish. Kominski just grunted and hung up without bothering to argue.

At the trailer park, David turned into a dirt road which branched off into several trails dividing the mobile homes. Many of the families who lived here were legal residents, those fortunate enough to have acquired a green card which allowed them to work in the United States. Because it was early evening, the park was crowded with children playing, young men working on their cars, and young girls out for walks and hoping to catch the attention of the young men.

"Ay, querida, venga aqui," crowed a tee-shirted boy who looked to be about seventeen. He closed the hood of his car and leaned against it,

A fifteen-year-old girl, clad in shorts and halter top, giggled and flounced away.

"Do you know where I can find Juan Ortiz's home?" asked David slowing down next to the boy's Pontiac.

The boy looked at him sullenly and then jerked his head toward the old battered Silver Streak across the road. David understood the reason for the distrust. He and his friends were probably stopped weekly by a city policeman, county sheriff, or Border Patrol agent. Sometimes the stops were warranted, as in the cases involving drunk driving or speeding. Sometimes they weren't.

"Senor Ortiz?" David rapped on the door to the trailer.

"Quien es?"

"Officer De Vargas con la policia. Puedo entrar?"

"Si. Pasale."

Inside, the trailer was surprisingly neat considering that it was merely one large room. David could smell chiles simmering in a pot. He noted the colorful crucifix on the door, a framed picture of the Virgen de Guadalupe over the chest, and a small radio on a corner table which was tuned to a Mexican station.

"Donde esta su esposa?" David asked politely, noting a few feminine articles.

"Esta muerta. Hace seis anos."

The man's wife had been dead for six years, and he still had her shawl hanging over a chair, thought David. A good devoted husband and a decent man, not likely to telephone the police with lies. He made polite conversation for a few more minutes until he heard Kominski's Lexus pulling into the small driveway next to his police cruiser. David opened the door himself to admit the sergeant.

"De Vargas," said Kominski brusquely, nodding at the younger officer. "Is this the man who telephoned you?"

"Yes, sir. This is Juan Ortiz. He's a naturalized American citizen, and has lived in this trailer park for eleven years."

"What has he told you?" asked Kominski with ill-disguised impatience. He had no interest in the man's personal background.

"He was scrounging for tin cans as he always does to make a little extra cash. None of the neighbors have ever minded if he goes through their trash cans. Today he found these." David gestured toward the table where a woman's leather purse and a small revolver were placed.

"And they were found where?" Kominski's eyes glistened. It was as if he anticipated the answer.

Juan Ortiz interrupted with a flood of Spanish.

"What did he say?" demanded the investigator.

"He says that he found the items in the trash can behind the trailer of Hector Lopez. But he says he doesn't think that Hector put them there, because he never had anything to do with guns before. He says that Hector is a good boy."

"I'll just bet," snorted Kominski. "It's enough to pick him up and bring him in for questioning." Without bothering to thank Ortiz, Kominski pulled his cellular telephone from his coat pocket and dialed the police station. "Gary, get over to the Mesa Roadhouse and pick up Hector Lopez."

"I'd like to be there, sir, if you don't mind," said David.

"Just keep your yap shut. I know you have a lot of sympathy for these people, having grown up here and all. But they lie like dogs and they'd kill for a bone. He did it, all right."

Out of the corner of his eye, David noticed that Juan Ortiz was glaring at the investigator. Either Ortiz understood a lot more English than he admitted, or Kominski's blatant racism needed no translation, thought David. He really needed to be at the station for that interview.

Twenty minutes later, David was standing at the counter talking to Helen Sinclair, the night dispatcher who had just come in for her shift.

"Edna Grunderson told me that Shea Chan, you know Dorothy's daughter, came into her shop to buy something for the funeral. She looked so thin and pale, even though she's already seven months gone. Deep circles under her eyes. And she seemed to be really worried about money, was real careful with what she spent," said Helen, clucking her tongue and looking concerned. "It's just real awful what that young girl has been through."

David listened, hungry for any detail about Shea, but not learning anything really new. He suspected that Shea might be in some financial distress, because her young husband could not have had time to provide for her before he died. And it didn't seem that Dorothy left a whole lot except for that old house and a bunch of antiques. His thoughts about Shea were interrupted when he Gary Armstrong ushering in a hand-cuffed Hector Lopez.

"Have you read him his rights?" asked Kominski, emerging from an inner office.

"Yes," answered Gary. "And we've already got his prints from the other day."

"Take him in there," said Kominski gesturing to the interrogation room at the end of the hallway.

"As if I didn't know," muttered Gary to David as he passed by with Lopez. "We black folks is just so dumb."

David started to smile at Gary's passable imitation of Kominski's New Jersey accent, but he immediately stopped when the front door opened to admit an hysterical young, Hispanic girl who was carrying a baby and followed by two small children.

"Lydia, vayase," yelled Hector as he was led down the hallway. Gary paused to allow Hector to speak to his wife. "No diga nada."

"I asked her to come down here," said Kominski. "We had a very interesting telephone call from the police department over in Alpine. It seems that Mrs. Lopez was not with you as you said on the morning that Dorothy O'Daniels was killed. She was in Alpine with the kids. The police know, because they stopped her later that morning on Highway 52 for an expired registration sticker. She told them then that she had been visiting with her sister in Alpine since Saturday. You don't have an alibi, boy, and you'd better start talking. David, you get Mrs. Lopez' statement and translate it. And tell her she'd better not make up any more stories." He turned to Hector, who looked as if he was about to break down. "We're going to be interviewing everybody who lives in that trailer park. And if nobody saw you in your trailer at precisely 2:35 a.m., then your ass is grass."

"I was just driving around town, having a couple of beers," shouted Hector.

"Why didn't you say that before?" asked Kominski, obviously enjoying Hector's discomfort.

"I'm from Mexico. I could lose my license just for that. And I knew you wouldn't believe me anyway."

"You got that right," said Kominski, following Hector and Gary into the interrogation room and slamming the door.

David walked over to his desk and turned on the computer. Lydia Lopez still stood, grief-stricken and staring at the door which had just imprisoned her husband.

"Senora," said David gently, "Sientase, por favor. Y digame todo."

Slowly the young woman lowered herself into the hard wooden chair and began to speak softly in Spanish.

On Thursday morning, Shea woke up feeling sluggish and tired. She had spent all day Tuesday and Wednesday preparing for the ceremonies planned for Thursday and Friday. Yesterday she had ordered wine and brandy from the University Beverage Store and flowers from Alana's Flowers and Gift Shop for the funeral parlor, church, graveside ceremony, and for the funeral reception. She and Berta had planned a menu for the reception, which included the traditional chicken mole. While Berta cooked, she ran the sweeper through the first floor rooms and dusted the furniture.

These activities had exhausted her so much that she had fallen right into bed without a thought for dinner. She slept through the night in a dreamless stupor and woke in the morning only when she smelled the coffee that George was preparing in the kitchen. After showering and changing into a pair of knit shorts and top, she went downstairs to have her daily allowance of caffeine, one cup.

"I miss this more than anything," said Shea as she practically inhaled the liquid. Her doctor in Arizona had strictly warned her against alcohol, which was no problem, and too much caffeine, which was a problem. She accepted the bacon and eggs that George put in front of her. "I'm definitely a caffeine addict."

"That means you're Dorothy's granddaughter for sure," said George. "She couldn't get enough of the stuff." He glanced at her sideways as if unsure how to broach the next subject. "We got a call from Chief Cummings while you were asleep. They think they've got the murderer."

"Who is it?" Even as she asked the question, Shea could feel her stomach
churning.

"They found Dorothy's purse and the gun that shot her in a trash can out back of Hector Lopez's trailer. It turns out he don't got no alibi for that morning. He was all alone. And they didn't find Dorothy's billfold or any money."

"That doesn't mean that he killed her. Dorothy couldn't have had that much money in her wallet. What, maybe two hundred dollars or so?"

Shea frowned at her coffee cup. She didn't know Hector all that well, but
Dorothy had always spoken well of him. Would he risk his job or kill someone for something as paltry as a couple of hundred dollars?

"Yeah, that's probably right. But maybe Hector thought he could get a little more out of the cash register. Maybe he didn't know she had already locked it and set the timer. You know, cooks don't make all that much, and he has three little kids. I bet he needed some money."

Before Shea could reply, Berta came bustling into the kitchen with groceries in her arms. She had been shopping for ingredients to make chile verde and chicken mole for the reception which would be held after the funeral.

"Ay Dios mio," she exclaimed as she put down her groceries. "I'm going to kill that Marlene Jankovitch myself. She keeps coming over here to help, wanting to pack up Miss O'Daniel's things, and she just messes things up."

Shea and George exchanged a smile. Berta was very territorial about the house, her kitchen, and Dorothy's clothes. For years, she had not only cleaned and cooked for Dorothy, but had taken her clothes to the cleaners, washed her fine lingerie, and mended her dresses.

"Shea, I found an old photograph album that belonged to Miss O'Daniels. I think she was looking at it the day before she died. Anyway I put it in your room in the top of your closet before that

Marlene can move it to where we'll never find it."

"Thanks, Berta," said Shea. "I'd like to take a look at it later. You know my grandmother used to keep all kinds of things in that old album, like my graduation invitations, newspaper clippings, little momentoes. If it meant something special, that's where she would keep it."

"Berta, did you hear about Hector Lopez?" interrupted George.

"Yes, I did, old man, and I don't believe a word of it. Hector thought the world of Miss O'Daniels. He was always telling her to be careful at the restaurant and offering to stay behind to help her lock up. Now why would he suddenly go and kill her for a little money?"

Why indeed? thought Shea. "Is there anyone to post bond for Hector?"

"I think our church, Immaculate Conception, is taking up a collection. I'm going to go by later and make a donation," said Berta. "But right now we have a lot to do. Your mother and sister are arriving tonight, mi hija, and I've got to get those rooms ready for them."

"We can put my mother in grandmother's room," suggested Shea. "I guess Megan could stay in the study. It still has a day bed in there."

In one of the back bedrooms, the moving company had left her desk, chair and computer equipment which she had yet to assemble. Until a few days ago, it had been Joe's sewing room, but George had already removed the machine and cutting table to the attic. The other back room was empty except for an old oak chest and rocking chair. Joe had told Shea she wanted to convert that room into a nursery for the baby.

"It will do," said Berta firmly. "We're not a hotel. And I don't want you running your feet off. You did way too much yesterday, and you still have to go to the funeral parlor for Visitation Hours, and you have to go to the Rosary tonight."

"I'll get over to the airport and pick up your folks," said George who was perusing the newspaper at the butcher block table. "They'll be gettin' in while you're at the Rosary. Do you mind if I drive Dorothy's truck? I'm havin' some problems with that old Dodge of mine."

"Not at all," said Shea. Dorothy had left behind a new red Ford pickup which, Jason Tyler had informed her, had been bought with cash. That must have pretty well depleted her bank account, thought Shea, who had yet to be informed of Dorothy's finances. That would be covered in the Reading of the Will, Mr. Tyler had told her. Maybe I'll get the truck and I can resell it for cash, Shea thought and then suffered the pangs of a guilty conscience. It seemed that lately all she thought about was money.

"Well, look at that," said George. "Nobody's claimed that big lottery. They got two more weeks and then that money goes right back into the pot."

"I better go home and check my lottery ticket again," said Berta with a laugh.

"Maybe I read the numbers wrong."

"Me, too," said George. "I'm gettin' so old, I think a six is a nine sometimes."

Shea didn't even want to think about it. She left the kitchen to go upstairs and put on her best maternity pant outfit, a pair of dark grey slacks and a dove grey henley top which she had bought for her graduation ceremony. She would wear this for both the Visitation and the Rosary. As she combed her hair she wondered fleetingly what David De Vargas thought about Hector Lopez as a suspect. He probably knew him if he'd been on the force for a while. If she saw him today or tomorrow, she decided she would ask his opinion.

Shea drove downtown and parked her car in the public parking space which surrounded the town square. The old-fashioned plaza, filled with benches, swings, and winding paths, served as both a city park and a public meeting space. A large white gaze-bo, which dominated the middle of the square, had served for over one hundred years as a platform for campaign speeches, evening concerts, and the occasional wedding reception. In better times, Shea could remember attending Independence Day picnics and Saturday night movies set up on a large portable screen in the park. People could buy popcorn and cotton candy from various Ladies Guilds which represented almost every church in town. Those were happier days spent with her grandmother whom she sorely missed at that moment.

With a small sigh she turned in the direction of the funeral par-lor which was a block away on Second Street. As she entered the red brick building, she heard the soft strains of Bach's "Jesu, Joy of Man's Desiring" coming from a sound system. It was one of the pieces which she had requested. Joe had known nothing about music until Shea, who had been a violinist in her high school orchestra, had introduced her to some of the classics. The next piece, she recalled from her conversation with William MacKenzie, would be Albinoni's "Adagio in G Minor". It was a haunting, intense piece of music and one which her grandmother had particularly

31

liked. At a walnut desk near the entrance to the viewing room, Shea saw registry books and pens waiting for the expected visitors. From an office to the side, William MacKenzie appeared with his usual unobtrusive manner.

"Good morning, Mrs. Chan," said the funeral parlor director with a small smile.

"Please call me Shea. Everyone else in the town does."

"It would be my pleasure. Would you like to see your grandmother?"

He led Shea to the brightly-polished oak coffin which was surrounded by arrangements of white carnations and yellow daisies, Joe's favorite flower. For the first time she was able to look at her beloved Joe without breaking into tears. It seemed that in the past few days she had depleted her reservoir of tears and would need time to replenish that source. Perhaps that was the purpose of all these funereal customs, thought Shea. It was to force the grieving to deal with the everyday necessities of life. Otherwise one could simply go mad with sorrow.

"We have a seating arrangement for you over here, my dear." MacKenzie waved a hand at the deep red sofa and the two print armchairs grouped around a coffee table in a separate alcove. On the table was a silver coffee urn, fueled by candle power, a silver creamer and sugar pot, and several china cups and saucers. "We ordered decaffeinated coffee for you. But if you need tea or juice or anything, please don't hesitate to ask. You will be here for a few hours, and we don't want you to be overtaxed."

Shea settled on the sofa and poured a cup of the dreaded decaf. Not bad, she thought after the first sip. Listening to the music, she relaxed for the first time in days. Strange, she thought, that being in this room with her grandmother would bring her a feeling of peacefulness. Her reverie was interrupted when the first visitors came quietly into the room. Walking softly, as if they might awaken the sleeping Dorothy, the two women and one man practically tiptoed over to the coffin. Shea recognized Marlene and Bob Crockett, the hefty, ruddy-faced morning cook of the Mesa Roadhouse. The other woman, a young Hispanic girl, must be a daytime waitress.

"She looks real good, don't she?" said Bob.

"Yes, she does, mighty good. I picked out that suit for her," said Marlene.

"It looks good with her fair skin," said the young girl. "She was a real nice lady."

"Hello, sweetie, I didn't see you sitting there," said Marlene suddenly spying Shea sitting quietly in the corner. She walked over and enveloped Shea in her arms. "How are you darling?"

"I'm fine, Marlene. How are all of you?"

"Not so good, honey," said Marlene with flashing eyes. "We can't believe that no good Yankee, Aaron Kominski, arrested Hector. A sweeter boy never lived. He couldn't possibly have murdered Dorothy."

"I wish I had the money to post all his bail, but I'm kinda short on funds right now," said Bob, looking a little sheepish. "I had a mortgage payment on my motorcycle come due this week. And I got another one next week on my boat. But still I'm going over to the church and put a little money in the pot."

"Me, too. I'm Cecilia De Anda," said the young girl. "I also work at the Mesa Roadhouse."

"Well, excuse me for my bad manners," interrupted Marlene. "I would forget my own head if it wasn't glued on. Shea, this is Ceci. She just started working here a year ago when she graduated from high school. Do you remember Rosie, Ceci's older sister? She's a couple of years younger than you. These are real good girls," said Marlene putting her arm around Ceci. "They both take care of their sick mom at home. She's got cancer, you know." Marlene had let her voice drop as if by doing so Ceci would be unable to hear her.

"That must be really hard on you," said Shea with feeling. The music system had begun to play "Fantasia on a Theme by Thomas Tallis."

"It kinda is. Rosie works the morning shift from six until two, and I work the later shift from two until ten. That way my mom always has one of us with her, and we don't have to pay for a nurse's aide."

"Still it's real expensive for these gals," said Bob. "You know none of us get insurance benefits with this job. We all have to pay for our own policies. And the girls have a lot of medications to pay for."

"Now be fair, Bob," said Marlene, always eager to stick up for the underdog.
"Leland would pay us better benefits, but his businesses ain't been doing so good these past few years. I think he's losing a good bit of money."

Shea knew that she was referring to Leland Johannson, the owner of the restaurant and several other small businesses around town, including Johannson's Market on Main Street and Johannson's Grain and Feed on Highway 52.

"Well, we got to get going," Marlene was saying. She hooked

her arm through Bob's ample limb. "Leland gave us all a little time off to come to this thing, but we got to get back. But first we're all going over to the church and give a little bit for Hector. He needs all the help and support he can get. What that smarty-pants detective don't know is that in small towns we stick together."

For the rest of the afternoon until three o'clock, there was a steady stream of visitors. Business owners, school teachers, farmers, and truck drivers came by to offer their heart-felt condolences to Shea. Some of them she remembered from her summer vacations as a child, and some of them were strangers. Several truckers remarked that she was the nicest lady on their route, and they always stopped for coffee and pie whenever they came close to Mesa.

"You knew that you would always get a good piece of pie and a good conversation whenever Dorothy was working," said one bearded driver of indeterminate age. "She talked about you quite a bit. And you're every bit as pretty as she said."

While the truck drivers talked about Dorothy's good qualities, most of the townies concentrated on the breaking news of the day, Hector's arrest. Like her first visitors, almost everyone believed that he was innocent.

At four o'clock she finally managed to straggle home, eat a ham sandwich and fruit salad left for her in the refrigerator by Berta, and lay down for a nap. Unfortunately sleep eluded her, and she kept thinking about the conversations she had held with various people that day. This evening she would see many of the same people at the rosary. Noone seemed to believe that the young cook could have killed his co-worker. The question was, if he didn't do it, who did? No clues had emerged which pointed to transients or hobos, the first group suspected of the crime. That left the extremely possible alternative that the murderer could be someone that Dorothy knew.

Shea shuddered at the thought. Could someone who had just professed sadness at Joe's death be the one actually responsible for it?

Berta's Mole Sauce

2 medium green peppers
1 medium quartered onion
1/4 cup almonds
1/4 cup peanuts
1/4 cup raisins
1 large clove garlic, diced
1/2 cup tomatoes

1/4 cup croutons
3/4 cup tortilla chips
2 cups water
1/4 vegetable oil
1/4 cup chocolate chips
Salt

1. Blend together croutons and chips. Empty into mixing bowl.
2. Blend together diced peppers, onions, almonds, peanuts, raisins, garlic, tomatoes.
3. Mix ingredients. Fry in pan with oil.
4. Add 2 cups water. Stir until mole is thick. Remove from heat.
5. Add chocolate chips and salt
6. Serve over baked chicken which has been shredded into small pieces.
7. Serve with rice or beans.

Spanish/English Translation

Ay querida. Venga aqui. Hey sweetheart. Come over here.

Quien es? Who is it?

Officer De Vargas con la policia. Officer De Vargas with the police.

Puedo entrar? May I come in?

Si. Pasale. Yes. Come in.

Donde esta su esposa? Where is your wife?

Esta muerta. Hace seis anos. She is dead. For six years.

Lydia, vayase. No diga nada. Lydia, go away. Don't say anything.

Senora, sietase por favor. Senora, please sit down.

Y digame todo. And tell me everything.

La Mesa Noticia, Friday, June 7

Personal and Want Ads

Busboy needed at the Mesa Roadhouse. Contact Marlene Jankovitch at 555-4040.

Typesetter wanted. Call *La Mesa Noticia*.

Anyone with information concerning a runaway Boxer should contact the City Health Department. It may be a rapid hog.

Single African-American male wishes to meet single African-American female. Must love jazz. Contact the Mesa Police Department.

(Editor's Note: Tuesday's editorial should have read, "Next summer marks the *120th* anniversary" not the "*1,120th* anniversary.")

CHAPTER THREE

"Two hundred thousand dollars bail," thundered the judge as he pounded his gavel on the table.

"All rise," said the bailiff as Judge John Ayes, a forty-year-veteran in district court, left the room. Old, wizened, and world-weary, he was seldom questioned in his decisions. Jessica Gutierrez, Hector's attorney who was providing her services pro bono, gave her client a look of resignation.

"I'm sorry, Mr. Lopez," she said before the bailiff reached for him. As he passed by David De Vargas, who had just testified about finding Dorothy's body, Hector tried to smile and failed miserably.

"There's no way of getting the bail reduced?" David asked the pretty, young attorney who just shook her head.

"With 'Honest Ayes'?" she remarked glumly, referring to the judge's nickname among the courtroom lawyers. "No such luck, David." Glancing at her watch, she mumbled a hasty goodby, grabbed her briefcase and rushed from the room.

"Are you going to the funeral, David?" Patrolman Hank Hatfield had walked into the courtroom wearing his uniform. As usual his curly red hair stuck out in all directions.

"Yeah, I think I can just make Mass."

"Nice suit," said Hank, admiring the dark blue single-breasted suit and burgundy striped tie.

"Only suit."

The courthouse was three blocks away from the church on a quiet street which was also occupied by the Mesa Public Library and Mesa Elementary School. He arrived at St. Francis Chuch just in time to see the black Cadillac limousine, furnished by MacKenzie Funeral Home, pull up in front of the church. He watched as the driver, barely more than a teenager, got out, opened the back door, and helped three women from the car. Shea was the first. Even in her advanced stage of pregnancy, David thought she looked great in a navy striped suit and navy hat with a veil which covered her eyes. An older, well-groomed woman

with pale blonde hair and wearing a dark pant suit was next.
She must be Shea's mother, he decided. Finally a young woman, a few years older than Shea, exited the vehicle. Wearing a short black leather skirt which reached to her mid-thigh and a black leather jacket over a tight lacy blouse, she took the driver's hand as she climbed from the back seat, shook her blonde hair which showed dark roots and gave him a dazzling smile.

David remembered Megan O'Daniels from the times she had visited with her sister at her grandmother's home. A year older than himself, she had seemed light years ahead when it came to sexual awareness. Although he was fairly sure that most of the stories which the other boys told about her were fictional, David had still been intrigued by her complete confidence in her ability to captivate the opposite sex. At the moment, the driver seemed unsure what he was supposed to do next, whether it was to wait in the car or fly to the moon. David was sure he would do either for Megan.

Following the family at a respectful distance, he took a seat a few rows behind the front pew on the opposite side. This location afforded him a good view of Shea and her relatives. As he knelt to say his opening prayers, he could see Shea doing the same, but her mother and sister remained seated. He remembered vaguely hearing that they were not Catholic. Apparently Shea had adopted her father's religion.

Throughout the first two readings, David's eyes continued to wander in the direction of Shea's pew. As the congregation stood for the gospel reading, he noticed that she seemed a little slow in rising and that she put a hand on her side. Even Father Jim, often David's jogging partner on Sunday afternoons, glanced over at Shea with some concern before he began the passage from St. John.

"This is the word of the Lord," he intoned at the end.

"Praise to You, Lord Jesus Christ," murmured the parishioners in response.

"Dorothy Josephine O'Daniels was a remarkable woman," began Father Jim. "She was born, Dorothy Smithers, right here in Mesa, Texas in 1924. As a child, she lived through the Great Depression and helped out on her parents' farm with her two older brothers. She was a teenager when the second world war broke out and ready to graduate from high school. That was when Patrick O'Daniels, also 18, decided that they should marry. He was ready to enlist in the military, but he wanted to ensure that she would be by his side. She was the prettiest and sweetest girl in town, he told people, and he wanted her for his wife.

So they married, and she waited for four long years while he fought in North Africa, was trained as a paratrooper in England, and then participated in the invasion of Normandy. Dorothy did her part for the war at home, working in a defense factory in Amarillo. When the war ended, Patrick returned to work at his father's construction business, O'Daniels Building Company. Patrick and Josephine wanted a family, and soon they had a son, Robert. Dorothy stayed home in their small bungalow on the north side of town to care for her child and the other children they hoped to have. Unfortunately this dream was not to be realized. They were destined to have no more children. Dorothy was dealt another tragedy when Patrick was only 42. He died unexpectedly of a heart attack, leaving Dorothy a young widow. Robert finished college at Texas Tech, received a job with Texas Instruments in Dallas, and Dorothy moved into the O'Daniels house to care for her ailing mother-in-law. To help with the family finances, now that O'Daniels Building Company had been sold, Dorothy took a job waitressing at the Mesa Roadhouse. For the next thirty-two years, Dorothy's life was a mixture of vinegar and honey. She buried her mother-in-law twenty-five years ago. Then she buried her only son ten years ago. He left behind two young daughters, Megan and Shea."

Father Jim paused, and David realized that he had diplomatically not mentioned the divorce that had occurred between Robert and Lisa O'Daniels ten years before his death. Lisa O'Daniels, he noticed, looked tense and angry. She stared implacably at the priest, hardly noticing that her oldest daughter was in tears.

"Yet despite her losses and her pain, Dorothy lived a full life. She doted on her two beautiful grandaughters who visited her almost every summer. She loved her job at the restaurant where she regularly served both loyal townspeople and grateful strangers. She listened to their stories, dispensed advice, rejoiced in births, and grieved over deaths.

Dorothy never failed to bake cupcakes for the church bazaars or sew costumes for the Christmas pageants. She delighted in playing bingo every week at St. Francis Church, she loved watching the Dallas Cowboys, and she even had fun buying the occasional lottery ticket. Her joy was in the simple pleasures of life. And she will be sorely missed."

The young priest returned to his chair where, as was the custom after homilies, he remained in thoughtful prayer for a moment. It was a simple and eloquent memorial, David thought as he watched tears streaming down the cheeks of Megan O'Daniels. For the life of him, he couldn't remember her married name. Or was she divorced now?

It didn't surprise him that she was crying. Megan and Shea had both loved their grandmother who had showered them with homecooked meals, trips to the rodeo and movie theatre, and provided a warm home that was always filled with friends. David wondered if they had the same atmosphere in their home in Dallas. Glancing again at Lisa O'Daniels, he doubted it.

During Communion, which arrived quicker than usual since a funeral Mass contained no collection ceremony, he followed his row up to the altar to receive the Host from Father Jim. On his return, he was able to glimpse a bit of Shea's face under the veil and was shocked to see how pale she looked, even worse than the last time he had seen her.

I'm going to have to keep a close eye on her today, he thought. She doesn't look well.

This sun is unbearable, thought Shea for the third or fourth time that morning. While listening to Father Jim perform ablutions at her grandmother's graveside, Shea felt oddly uncomfortable. She shifted on her feet and wished that she had someone to hold her hand, more for balance than for comfort. Megan was still weeping softly, and Lisa had her arm around her shoulders. The priest said the final prayer, people crossed themselves and genuflected, and then the crowd began to disperse toward parked cars. Shea, who was walking behind Megan and Lisa, stumbled a little.

"Would you like some help?"

Shea felt someone putting a hand under her elbow and looked up at the tall, young man who had materialized by her side.

"Thanks, Officer. I think the sun and heat are getting to me. It must be ninety degrees already."

"It probably is. I think we're going to have an early summer," said David easily.
"Have you been to see a doctor since you've been in town?"

"I haven't had time yet. I've been so busy with all these arrangements. But tomorrow I'm going to call Dr. Martin. Does he still practice?"

"Yes. His patients won't let him retire. He's been here forever. Not only was he my mother's doctor when I was born, but he was also her mother's doctor when she was born."

"Thank you, Officer," said Shea as they reached the limousine. "I hope that we see you at the reception."

As she was being helped into the car, Megan turned to see whether or not the male escorting her sister was presentable. Apparently David passed the test, because she sent him a provocative sidelong glance.

"Who was that?" she asked Shea in the limousine.

"David De Vargas," was Shea's curt response.

"Well, he certainly turned out nice. Tall, cute and lots of sex appeal."

Lost in her own thoughts, Shea didn't reply. The funeral had brought back memories of Mark whose loss was still so deeply felt. At the house, she hurried to the kitchen where Berta and George, who had skipped the graveside ceremony, were busy with last minute preparations.

"Why don't you go lie down for awhile?" scolded Berta.

"It makes me feel better to stay busy," replied Shea. She took a couple of platters and placed them on the dining table. As she entered the dining room, she could tell from the smell that her mother, a dedicated chain smoker, was seated across the foyer in the parlor. Last night Lisa and Megan had arrived while Shea was at the Rosary. Megan had chosen her grandmother's bedroom and was already asleep while Lisa confiscated Shea's room.

"I don't want to be any bother," her mother had said in a tone of martyred resignation which meant, if you throw me out, you'll burn in hell.

So Shea had slept in the study on the day bed which had worn springs and a lumpy mattress. Maybe that was why her back was hurting so much today. For comfort, she had taken Dorothy's old photo album to bed with her. She decided that she would begin with the first page, taking her time to peruse the volume, and enjoying fond memories along the way. Before she fell asleep, she put the album in her backpack. Because the study was crammed with boxes of Dorothy's clothes which had been sorted and packed by Marlene, Shea decided to place her backpack in the trunk of her car. She was really afraid that Marlene, who seemed to be on a mission for the angel of discarded clothes, might donate her backpack to the Goodwill by mistake along with her grandmother's things.

"Dorothy looked lovely."

"She had a great life didn't she? What a gutsy lady."

"I hope I have that kind of a turnout when I die. Half the town was at the funeral."

41

"What's in these cookies, anyway? Does Alberto use ginger in everything?"

As Shea wandered from room to room, accepting condolences from dozens of people, she caught snatches of conversation. Spying David De Vargas standing next to Chief Beau Cummings, she smiled at them both, but didn't have the time to talk to them. At the same time she noticed that Megan was being monopolized by Leland Johansson. Although he was quite a bit older and at least three times divorced, Megan didn't seem to notice. She smiled and dimpled as the balding, spectacled, somewhat frumpy businessman spoke to her in low, serious tones.

"Could you tell me where the bathroom is?"

Shea turned around to see Ceci De Anda, standing next to her sister, Rosie. They are very pretty girls, she thought, if a little on the thin and serious side.

"We only have one," said Shea. "It's right upstairs."

While carrying a glass of chablis to Father Jim, she heard her mother speaking to Marlene Jankovitch.

"Haven't we met before?" her mother was saying.

"No, I don't think so, honey."

"I'm sure we have. Have you ever been to Dallas?"

"No, not that I can recall." Did Marlene sound a little impatient? thought Shea. Well, her mother was being awfully persistent.

"Perhaps it was in Las Vegas. Do you ever go there?"

Shea couldn't hear Marlene's answer, because she was suddenly confronted by an outraged Berta.

"I had to run that big hulk of a man, Bob Crockett, out of the kitchen. He was going through drawers. Claimed he was looking for a knife to cut the ham that Edna Grunderson brought. Who asked him to do that? I take care of the kitchen!"

After placating the distraught housekeeper, Shea finally managed to find a chair and sank into it gratefully. When David took the empty chair next to her and handed her a china cup filled with hot tea, she didn't even object.

"I just spoke with Dr. MacKenzie over there," he said indicating a tall, slender and very striking woman dressed in a black silk sheath. "She said that a cup of herbal tea couldn't hurt you and would probably do you a world of good."

"She's really beautiful, isn't she?" asked Shea in admiration. She didn't know how anyone could be so poised and polished.

"Yes, she is," said David who was not looking at Vanessa MacKenzie.

Shea watched as Megan approached Vanessa and seemed to

introduce herself. Although she couldn't hear Vanessa's responses, she could clearly understand Megan's high-pitched tone as her sister asked the much taller woman if she remembered her from a Miss Dallas Beauty Pageant. Apparently Vanessa, who appeared almost nonchalant about the event, had been one of the finalists. Megan, Shea vaguely remembered, had not made it past the initial rounds despite the fact that she had spent a great deal of money on her gown, hairstyle, and makeup.

"My goal was always to earn scholarship money so that I could attend medical school," Vanessa was saying. Because of a fortunate lull in the room, Shea was able to overhear her well-modulated tones. "I never liked pageants that much although I really liked the other girls."

Megan simply looked at her, mystified.

"Excuse me, I'd like to speak to your sister. I haven't had the opportunity to meet her yet," said Vanessa graciously as she walked away from Megan.

"Hi, Vanessa," said David standing up when she approached them. "This is Shea Chan."

"Hello, Shea. I knew your grandmother very well. We used to hang out at the Roadhouse when I was a student at Mesa State. She gave us great hamburgers and even greater advice. She was very much loved around here."

"Thank you," said Shea. She had heard it often that afternoon, but Vanessa said it the most sincerely. "I understand that you are a pediatrician."

"Yes, I am," said Vanessa with the smile that must have been responsible for her beauty pageant success, "and you look like you might need one." Suddenly her smile turned into a slight frown. "As a matter of fact, you are looking a little peaked. Don't you think you should lie down?"

"When all of this is over, I promise I will do that. Berta and George have been nagging at me all afternoon. But we still have to go through with the Reading of the Will when the reception is done."

"Then maybe we can help you clear the room a bit," said David. He commandeered Beau Cummings, and together they began to quietly urge people to leave. Shea knew she shouldn't have allowed it, but she was far too tired to deal with any more visitors.

"Do you think we can get on with this thing?" Her mother had suddenly appeared, cigarette in hand, to stand before her. "Megan and I have to catch a plane back to Dallas tonight."

"We can begin right now if you like." Jason Tyler spoke quiet-

43

ly but with authority. "Could we have everyone in the living room, please?"

Remembering what he had said about this particular ceremony, Shea went to the walnut entertainment unit which covered an entire wall opposite the sofa. In addition to a large color television, there were rows of shelves and some closed cabinets. One of these cabinets held an extensive liquor collection including Bailey's Irish Cream, Christian Brothers Brandy, and Bushmill Scotch. While she chose a bottle of brandy, George carried in a silver tray with four Waterford crystal brandy snifters on it. Berta rolled in the mahogany tea cart, laden with a sterling silver antique tea set, delicate china cups and plates, and a platter of biscochos.

After everyone had picked their beverage of choice, they settled into leather chairs or on the sofa. Marlene and Lisa chose the sofa with Megan positioned between them while Jason sat in one of the leather club chairs. Shea and Berta occupied the other two chairs, and George stood.

"This is the last will ever made by Mrs. O'Daniels," began Jason. "It was witnessed by Alice Tyler and myself. The date of the will is the last day of December." He shot Shea a meaningful glance, and she steeled herself to hear that she was suddenly homeless again.

"To my friend and longtime housekeeper, Berta Rivera, I leave my collection of Hummel figurines."

Berta gasped and then reached for her handkerchief. She dabbed at her eyes.

"She enjoyed so many hours of dusting and caring for them, that she deserves this collection, to do with as she chooses." Jason stopped reading and beamed at Berta. "I know that this collection has great sentimental value for you, but if you wish to have it appraised, I would recommend it. These figurines are worth possibly thousands of dollars."

Berta, speechless for once, only nodded.

"To my husband's oldest friend and also my true friend, George Fallchurch, I leave my new Ford truck, recently purchased. I also stipulate that George will be given rent-free lodgings over the garage for as long as he chooses to live there."

Jason handed an envelope which contained the car title to the handyman.

Accepting it reluctantly, George looked shocked and then glanced at Shea, slightly embarrased at the largesse of his friend. She shook her head at him as if to say, don't worry about it.

"To my dear friend, Marlene Jankovitch, with whom I have

44

enjoyed so many hours of bingo, I leave a momento of my husband's devotion, my twentieth anniversary diamond ring."

"That dear woman," exclaimed Marlene. She accepted the ring, wrapped in white tissue, from Jason while Lisa O'Daniels' eyes shot daggers at the waitress. Marlene, her own eyes downcast and unreadable, didn't seem to notice.

"To my daughter-in-law, Lisa O'Daniels, I leave my Cartier watch," continued Jason.

When Jason handed her the tissue-wrapped watch, Lisa didn't even react, but Shea could see a faint sneer at the corner of her mouth. Although it was not as expensive as the ten thousand dollar diamond anniversary ring, it was still a very generous gift, considering that Lisa hadn't spoken to her mother-in-law since the divorce from her son.

"To my granddaughter, Megan, and my great granddaughter, Shannon, so that they will be provided for in years to come, I name them as beneficiaries of my life insurance policy worth two hundred fifty thousand dollars."

Both Megan and Lisa cried out at once and hugged each other. When they had calmed down, Jason continued.

"Actually it is worth more than two hundred thousand dollars. The policy had a clause for double indemnity. When a policyholder is murdered, the benefits are doubled. You will actually receive five hundred thousand dollars, Megan."

"Four hundred thousand . . ." Megan was too stunned to finish the sentence.

"I have forms prepared for you, and if you will just sign these, I can hand over a check today."

The pen was barely out of Jason's coat pocket before Megan grabbed it and scribbled on the legal document.

"What about Shea, Jason? Dorothy wouldn't forget her," growled George.

"I was just getting to that," said Jason smoothly. Dorothy might not have forgotten her granddaughter, he thought, but her mother certainly had. Lisa looked as if she had just been smacked in the face with a frying pan and could only stare at the check in Megan's hand.

"To my granddaughter, Shea and her husband Mark Chan . . ." Jason paused with a glance at Shea who was handling it very well. "I leave the O'Daniels Home and all the possessions in it. They will also have access to the family jewels which are kept in the First City Bank of Mesa. This will be their property for as long as they wish to keep the home. They are, however, forbidden to sell the property or dispose of the possessions within during their lifetime. Should they wish to forfeit the property, the house, jewels and furnishings will be deeded over to the county to be used as a museum. Upon the death of both parties, the house will pass to their heirs. If their heirs wish to forfeit the property, the same conditions apply."

Well, thought Shea with relief, at least I have a place to live.

"This provision does not apply to any funds or cash which may be available within the house or in the checking or savings account at the bank." Jason cleared his throat to continue and took a sip of his brandy. "I don't know if she had any cash in the house, Shea, but her combined checking and savings account listed $2,903.47. She had no outstanding debts and her property taxes have been paid for the remainder of the year. There are also some old stocks and bonds which I haven't appraised in years. We can take a look at those although I don't think they will be worth much."

"Thank you, Jason," said Shea. She wasn't exactly a pauper, but she was close to it. "Is there anything else?"

"There are some small bequests of bonds for Dorothy's two nieces and two nephews, the grown children of her two brothers. Each of them have sent flowers and telegrams with their regrets that they could not attend the funeral."

"I remember," said Shea. Apparently Dorothy's only surviving brother had moved to Australia after the war, and his children still lived there. "They sent two beautiful wreaths with white roses, didn't they?"

"Yes," said Jason. "That was from the Smithers."

Lisa and Megan had disappeared upstairs, presumably to pack for their return journey. George had been drafted to drive them to the airport, and he was looking none too happy about it.

"I don't mean to complain, Shea, but that mother of yours smokes like a chimney," he said. "Smells up that new truck somethin' awful."

"They're sure eager to get home and start spending that money," whispered Berta in an undertone to George while Shea was seeing Jason to the door.

"Ain't they?" he agreed.

Marlene, overhearing their exchange, winked at them like a co-conspirator.

"Hey, sweetie," she said to Shea. "Are you going to be all right? You're not looking so good."

"I'll be okay, Marlene. But thanks anyway."

At least she had asked, Shea thought. Her mother hadn't

inquired about her health all day. Although she hadn't eaten much, she felt queasy, as if she were having cramps from a bad piece of shrimp.

When everyone had left, Shea helped Berta clear dishes and leftover food from all the rooms. They had just finished loading the dishwasher when Shea suddenly bent over in pain.

"Ay Dios mio," cried Berta. "I knew something was wrong."

"I'll be okay in a minute," panted Shea. "I just need to catch my breath."

Before she could speak again, she felt a rush of warm water. In seconds she was standing in a liquid pool.

"Your water has broken, mi hija. Va. Se acabo. I'm calling for an ambulance," said Berta.

"I don't need an ambulance."

"You need someone to take you to the hospital right away, and that's not me. I can't drive."

"Call Marlene at the Roadhouse. See if there's anyone who could come for me." Shea headed for the stairs. "What I need is to change these clothes."

"Hola," said Berta. "Quien es? No esta Marlene? No. This is Berta Rivera. Well then, who is there? He is? Let me talk to him. Can you get over here right away? Her water broke. She has to go to the hospital now. Ahorale."

Upstairs, despite the seriousness of the situation, Shea felt oddly excited. She was at last going to have Mark's baby. Quickly changing into a more comfortable pair of pants and top, she packed a small bag with toiletries, nightwear, and clean underwear. She wished that she had taken the opportunity to buy a diaper bag and baby carrier as well as all the little layette things that new moms usually owned by now. No matter, she sighed. She would get around to that. Searching through her desk drawer for her CD player and some discs, which she wanted to use for a distraction during the early part of labor, she remembered that she had left those in her backpack. She went downstairs to the driveway and retrieved her backpack from the car just as David De Vargas drove up and parked.

"Are you okay? Do we have time to make it? Are you having contractions?" he asked in alarm.

"Calm down. You're more nervous than I am. I'm having some small contractions, but there is plenty of time. Why aren't you wearing your uniform?" she asked, noting that he was dressed in jeans and a white shirt.

"Even policemen get the night off occasionally. And it's a good thing, too. I was having dinner at the Roadhouse when Berta called. Are those the only bags you're taking?"

He picked up the small duffle bag and her backpack under the watchful eye of Berta.

"You drive her to the hospital real careful, you hear," she admonished. "And call me as soon as the baby is born. I'm staying right here until Shea comes home."

"Yes, ma'm."

On the way to the hospital, Shea was quiet, rubbing her stomach and breathing softly. David glanced over at her from time to time. She didn't seem in the least bit concerned.

"Are you scared?" he finally asked.

"Yes and no," she answered truthfully. "At my last prenatal visit at the University of Arizona, the obstetrician told me that at seven months pregnant a baby has an excellent chance of surviving birth without serious complications. And I must be a week or two beyond seven months. So I just have to pray for the best."

At Mesa Medical Clinic she was admitted with her insurance card, and the nurse on duty called Dr. Martin.

"Who is your pediatrician?" the nurse asked.

"I guess it's Dr. MacKenzie."

"She's the best. We'll have to call her as well, because the baby is going to be premature. If you'll come with us, we'll take you to a room."

"Goodby, David," she said as she sat in the wheelchair.

That's the first time she's called me by my name, he thought.

"Sir, if you'll come with us, we'll get you into some scrubs." When the young man looked at her blankly, the nurse said with some impatience, "Don't you want to help your wife with labor? Didn't you do the Lamaze classes?"

"Uh, sure, ma'm," said David in surprise. Why not? "Just tell me where to go."

In the O'Daniels foyer Berta used window cleaner and paper towels to clean the glass on the Biedermeyer cabinet which held the Hummel collection. It's almost a shame to take them from this house, she thought. They are so beautiful. Well, there is no rush. I need to buy a cabinet that locks just like this one, before I take these home.

When she heard the telephone ringing, she hurried into the

kitchen to answer the old oak wall phone.

"Bueno."

"Berta, it's me, George."

"Well, what's taking you so long? Shea had to go to the hospital. Her water broke. She's going to have the baby any time now."

"After I took those two women to the Alpine Airport, I ran over a nail and got a flat. The garage here had to call over to Davis for the right kind of tire, and it won't get here 'til the mornin'. So I just checked into a motel. I'm dead tired, and I'm going to leave tomorrow as soon as I can. I'll call the hospital to check on Shea. Who's with her anyway?"

"David De Vargas came over here to take her."

"David! You let David De Vargas take her."

"Oh, stop huffing and puffing, old man. I don't know what I would have done if he hadn't come along. You know I can't drive."

After hanging up the telephone, she went upstairs to make sure that the rooms were left in order. In the study, the daybed was neatly prepared, but in Shea's bedroom, occupied last by Lisa O'Daniels, Berta had to open the windows to clear out the stale air. Finally she entered Dorothy's bedroom and threw up her hands in disgust. The bed was unmade, drawers were open, and things had been thrown around the room. As she began to pick up and restore the mess, she kept up a constant strain of Spanish, blaming Megan O'Daniels, who was well-known for her untidiness.

After a moment, she fell silent as an uneasy sensation settled on her. Megan might have left the bed unmade, but why would she throw her grandmother's things around the room. As Berta looked more closely at the drawers, it appeared to her that someone had been rummaging in each one. Megan would have no reason to do that, she thought. She could have anything of her grandmother's that she wanted.

For an eerie second, Berta had the feeling that she was not alone in the house. She stood still, her heart pounding so loud she was sure that whoever stood just outside the bedroom must surely hear it. When the telephone rang again, she let out a shrill scream. She walked over to Dorothy's nightstand and picked up the receiver of the old-fashioned Country French telephone.

"Bueno," she managed to say in a whisper.

"Berta, are you all right? It's David. I'm at the hospital."

"How is Shea?"

"She just had the baby twenty minutes ago, ten minutes before midnight. A baby boy, four pounds. He's in the intensive care nursery."

49

"Is Shea all right?"

"She's doing fine. She's resting in her room right now. And I have some more good news for you. Someone posted bond for Hector Lopez. He was released a few hours ago."

"Gracias a Dios," said Berta happily.

"I'm going to be here all night. Will you be all right?"

"Of course," she said indignantly with more bravado than she actually felt.

Again hanging up the telephone, Berta decided to go downstairs and turn on the television in the living room. Miss O'Daniels had cable television, and she should be able to find a movie to watch. For some reason, she felt very skittish. Funny, she thought, she had never felt that way before in this house. Reaching the bottom of the stairs, Berta started to turn left. At that instance all the lights in the house went dark.

"Quien es? Who's there?" she called, peering into the dark hallway. Berta backed away slowly from the front door heading for the sanctuary of the kitchen and the back exit. She stopped when she heard another sound.
"George, is that you?"

Berta felt a sharp thud against the back of her head. By the time she fell to the floor, she felt nothing else.

Alberto's Biscochos
Mexican Wedding Cookies

6 1/2 cups flour

1 pound lard or shortening

2 sticks butter

1 t baking powder

1/2 t salt

1 cup sugar

1 egg

1/2 t vanilla

1 cup sugar and 5 t cinnamon mixed

1. In large mixing bowl cream lard or shortening and butter together.
2. Add milk, vanilla and unbeaten egg.
3. In separate bowl mix flour, sugar, salt, baking powder.
4. Add dry mixture to large mixing bowl a little at a time.
5. Press into shapes or use cookie cutter and place on greased cookie sheet.
6. Bake at 350 degrees for ten minutes.
7. While cookies are warm, roll them in sugar and cinnamon mixture.

Spanish/English Translation

Va. Se acabo. That's enough.

Ahorale. Right now.

Bueno. Hello.

Gracias a Dios. Thanks be to God.

From the *Obituary Column*

Dorothy Josephine O'Daniels, 74, died on Sunday, June 2 in Mesa, Texas. Mrs. O'Daniels, a life-long resident of the town, was married to Patrick O'Daniels, owner of O'Daniels Construction Company. Patrick O'Daniels was the descendant of one of the town's original settlers, Angus O'Daniels. Mrs. O'Daniels worked for thirty-two years at the Mesa Roadhouse.

The Visitation was held on Thursday from 12 to 3 p.m. at the MacKenzie Funeral Home. The Rosary was held that evening at 7 p.m. at St. Francis Church. The Funeral was held on Friday, June 8 at 10 a.m. Mrs. O'Daniels was buried next to her husband in Shady Grove.

Mrs. O'Daniels has survived her granddaughters, Megan O'Daniels Rilleux, 29, Shea O'Daniels Chan, 25, and her great-granddaughter, Shannon Rilleux, 9.

(Editor's Note: Friday's want ad should have read *"It may be a rabid dog"* NOT *"a rapid hog."*

CHAPTER FOUR

"He's absolutely perfect, isn't he?" Shea asked the nurse's aide. A grandmotherly type with salt and pepper hair, Mary O'Malley smiled in agreement. All the young mothers said that, no matter what their baby looked like.

This baby was actually quite pretty, thought Mary, noting the Asian features and small bones. Too bad the poor little thing was under an oxygen hut. He had been born six weeks early, and his lungs were still not fully developed. He also had the peachy fuzz of a premature baby and needed quite a bit of weight. Otherwise, though, he looked good.

"Have you named him yet, Mrs. Chan?"

"I'm naming him Mark after his father."

"I thought his father's name was David? I heard you calling him that in the delivery room." Even as she spoke, Mary knew she was making a faux pas. Today you never knew what went on with young couples.

"David is a friend of mine. Mark was my husband. He died four months ago."

"I'm so sorry," said the aide. She really didn't know what else to say, and she was afraid to ask too many questions. She could have sworn from the way that young man looked at her and was so concerned, well . . .

"I think I'll go back to my room," said Shea. "I need to call my mother and sister. They don't know about the baby yet."

Using her calling card, Shea called her mother's apartment in Dallas with no success. After reaching her Aunt Shirley, she learned that her mother, sister, and niece had taken a flight to Hawaii.

"That was quick," she said. "They just left here."

"Oh, they called me from the airplane and had me drive Shannon to the airport. When they arrived, they just bought tickets and took off for the islands. Isn't that exciting! I'll be sure and tell them about your baby boy, don't you worry."

Shea called Jerri next.

"Hello," mumbled a groggy voice.

"Hi, Jerri. This is Shea."

"Shea who?"

"Jerri, wake up. I know that it's only ten o'clock, but some people actually get up at a normal hour."

"I don't. I was at Gentle Ben's last night with a bunch of people from Dr. Johnson's class. Zach Hardaway and Vivian Diaz were there asking about you."

Shea flashed back to graduate school days and nights. Zach, Vivian, Jerri and she had taken several history graduate classes together, but she was the only one who continued to complete her Ph.D. Jerri had entered and graduated from law school, David had returned to a successful law practice, and Vivian had changed to an anthropology major. Gentle Ben's was a college hangout on University Avenue where they often congregated after a seminar or colloquium to have a few drinks, listen to the newest college band, and to discuss both academic and personal issues. Dr. Sydney Johnson had been one of their favorite professors, an elderly, scholarly history professor who was also a father-figure to many of them.

"I need to call both of them."

"Well, everybody wanted to know how you're doing in Mesa? How was the funeral for your grandmother? They're all very worried about you. They also want to know when you're going to return to Tucson."

"Not anytime soon, it seems," said Shea with a sigh as she continued to recall more care-free days spent researching at the university library and gossiping with her friends at Gentle Ben's. "That's why I'm calling. Last night after Joe's funeral, my water broke, and I delivered the baby. A little boy, four pounds. I named him Mark."

"Oh, my God." Jerri sounded fully alert now. "Tell me where you're staying. I'll let everybody know."

"It's at Mesa Medical Center," said Shea. She gave Jerri the address and telephone number.

"Shea?"

"Are you doing okay financially? I don't mean to be crass, but did your grandmother leave you anything?"

"I'm okay, Jerri. Actually she left me her house and furnishings. You know it's an historic house and full of antiques."

Jerri was quiet for a moment.

"Will you let me know if you need anything?"

Shea had to swallow hard before she answered. It was good

to have someone so concerned. "Yes, I will," she promised.

After finishing her call with Jerri, Shea called home for the third time that morning. That's really odd, she thought, as the phone rang and rang. I wonder why the answering machine is turned off. And where is Berta? Did she go to the grocery store? If so, it was taking her a very long time. Shea would have called Berta's apartment, but she didn't have the number.

Oh, well, thought Shea. She'll call in a little while. Berta had always been extraordinarily responsible.

Flowers had been arriving that morning as word of her baby's birth spread through the small town. Leland Johansson, owner of the Mesa Roadhouse, sent a vase of mixed spring flowers, and the Ladies Guild at St. Francis Church sent daisies for "Dorothy's new great-grandson."

A beautiful green vase held a dozen red roses which were Shea's favorite flower. The card which nestled in the baby's breath read simply "David." David De Vargas had been remarkably helpful last night, recalled Shea with a smile, and she had really appreciated him being there during the delivery. Only she thought she remembered once or twice calling him "Mark." Well, he was a good policeman and would make someone a good husband someday.

Shea wondered why Marlene hadn't called, and she telephoned the Mesa
Roadhouse to see if she could get Marlene's home telephone number.

"Mesa Roadhouse."

"Hello, this is Shea Chan. Is Marlene coming in today?"

"Oh, hi Shea. This is Rosie. How are you?"

"I'm just fine."

"How's the baby?"

"He's doing very well. He's still in intensive care and may be there for a few more days. His lungs still have to develop."

"Wow, we were so excited to hear about it. Ceci and I are coming over when our shift is finished. Oh, about Marlene. She's not coming in today. Bob invited her fishing after the funeral yesterday. They were both so depressed, he thought it would be a good idea to get away for awhile. I think they went to Silver Lake. He has a cabin up there."

"Does he have a telephone?"

"I don't think so." Shea could hear Rosie yelling a question at someone in the back. "No, he doesn't have a telephone."

"Who's cooking for the restaurant?" asked Shea with curiosity.

Rosie hesitated a fraction of a second. "Hector came in and said that he was flat broke. He asked if he could work today for whatever we could give him, even if it was just food for his family. I said I'd let him have my tips today. Just don't tell anyone. Leland Johannson might not like it."

Well, at least that was one good thing, thought Shea as she hung up. Hector would be taking home something. As soon as she had put down the receiver, it rang.

"Well, did you get your baby yet?"

"No, George, they told me I would have to wait a few more months. Of course, I "got" my baby," said Shea laughing. "He's in the intensive care nursery." She recited for the umpteenth time that morning all the vital statistics.

"Why ain't Berta answerin' the telephone?" was his next question.

"I don't know. Perhaps she went home to take care of something. She'll call. I know that she is dying to see the baby. When will you be here?"

"I'm still waitin' for that garage to find that blasted tire. Seems like they had to call another garage in Fort Stockton. I'm hopin' to be there before nightfall."

After hanging up the telephone, Shea decided to retrieve her CD player and some discs from her backpack. When she opened it, she realized the photograph album was in there. Pulling it from the backpack, she placed it on the cabinet which held the television and VCR with the intent of perusing it when she had time.

The hospital, which had been originally built in the 1920s of adobe, had been remodelled in recent years to reflect the modern needs of hospital patients. Peach, turquoise and mauve-trimmed curtains matched the same material that covered the two arm-chairs in the room. The same southwestern colors were repeated in the border which separated the ceiling from the walls and in the artificial flower arrangement located on the top of the light oak entertainment center. This was a far cry, thought Shea, from the hospital room in which she stayed when she had her tonsils removed at the age of ten.
Putrid green and aluminum were the fashion statements for those days.

Putting a disc into the player, Shea arranged the earphones and closed her eyes. Albinoni's "Adagio in G Minor" began its soothing musical therapy. Although it now reminded her of Joe lying in a coffin, she had always found comfort in the Baroque composition. Today, however, as she listened to the music, something oddly discordant struck her. It certainly wasn't the recording. It was just that the music, which had been played throughout Joe's Visitation, Funeral, and Reception, reminded her of something. Only she didn't know what. The nagging feeling remained throughout the nine-minute performance by the Academy of St. Martin-in-the-Fields.

A soft rap on her hospital door awoke her from her reverie. She opened her eyes to see Jason Tyler standing in the doorway holding by the handle a a long, white, wicker basket which was adorned on the hood with a powder blue silk bow. Like most women, Shea couldn't help but be cheered at the prospect of receiving a present, and she gave the lawyer a beaming smile. To her surprise, the usually reserved gentleman came over to her bed and gave her a warm hug.

"This is a treat," said Shea.

"When Lily heard that you had delivered, she sent our niece, Alice, to Edna's Boutique. You know that Edna also has sells infant items. I was afraid that you had not had the time to begin preparing a layette."

Which was a very delicate way of saying that Jason, more than anyone else, knew that her financial situation was precarious, thought Shea. She was grateful for his tact. And also for his, or Alice's, good taste.

"Oh, my goodness, look at this," she exclaimed, pulling various items from the basket. Soft cotton gowns, diaper shirts, booties, and receiving blankets, all in colors of blue, white, and yellow, filled the basket. There were even a couple of rattles and bottles for decorative purposes. At the bottom of the basket was a pastel print pad.

"Apparently this basket can also serve as a portable bassinette for the infant," said Jason who was struggling to understand the newest devices available for babies. "You know, for visiting friends and such."

"This is really too much, Mr. Tyler."

"Lily loved your grandmother, and you too, of course, very much. You know that she would be here if she could."

Shea nodded. Jason's lovely wife, Lily, had been confined to a wheelchair for some years. In addition to that, it was rumored that she had developed Alzheimer's disease and now seldom left their stately Tudor home. Jason stayed only a few minutes, but long enough to learn all the necessary details which he would later relay to his wife.

When the lawyer had left for a luncheon appointment at the

Alpine Country Club, Mary came bustling in with Shea's lunch tray.

"Don't you know that I saw that nice young man who came in with you last night downstairs in the gift shop?" she said as she placed the food on the turquoise-trimmed table.

"I hope he's not spending more money on me," said Shea with a frown.

Noticing that Shea was busy with her chile verde, Mary looked over at the red roses. That's interesting, she thought.

"I didn't know that your husband had died when I spoke to you last night," said Mary in a straight-forward yet sympathetic tone. "I'm new here."

"It's all right. I'm not really from here. I just came to visit my grandmother."

"She's the one who was killed in the restaurant?"

"Yes."

"It's a hard time you've been having, that's for sure," said Mary. All the while she was speaking, the aide was adjusting the bed, fluffing pillows, and removing the water pitcher to refill. "My husband also died when I was a young girl, back in Ireland."

Shea thought she had recognized a hint of Dublin.

"Did you come to America to work as a nurse's aide?" she asked to be polite.

"Oh, no. I've done many things. I was a taxi driver in New York for awhile, I waitressed in a San Francisco seafood restaurant, and I worked in a Chicago Hilton hotel as a maid. I took some nurse's training in Seattle. But I got tired of those big cities, don't you know. I was passing through Mesa, and it looked real nice. So I thought to meself, Mary, why don't you give it a go? And here I am."

"Do you still have family in Ireland?" asked Shea, truly intrigued by this rolling stone.

"Just a couple of brothers and sisters. Me mum and me da died years ago. And I never had children with Padraig. That's Celtic, you know for Patrick. You Yanks pronounce everything different. Hullo, there," she said interrupting her family history to greet the new visitor. "You'll be wanting to come in so don't dally. It's your young man," she said to Shea as she hurried from the room as if she were desperately needed to perform surgery.

"Hi," said David. He was wearing his uniform today, and in his hands he carried a fluffy, brown teddy bear.

"I guess that's for me," joked Shea.

"No, actually, it's for little Mark," he replied in the same tone. "I was down at the nursery, and one of the nurses brought his bassinette over to the window. He's still in an oxygen tent, but he's doing really well they tell me."

"He'll be on oxygen for some time, Dr. MacKenzie has said. She's really great. I think she will be here again a little later."

For a moment they fell silent. David sat in the armchair, fingering the teddy bear.

"I really haven't thanked you for everything you did," said Shea. "It was really far and beyond a policeman's duty."

David gave her a strange look. "It was all right. You must really be missing your husband."

"I am," whispered Shea, afraid that she would cry. In order to avoid that, she changed the subject. "Has anything new come up concerning Joe's investigation?"

"No, Kominski still believes that Hector is the number one suspect. He'll go to trial even though there's mostly circumstantial evidence against him."

"What I can't understand is the motive behind this. I mean, why would he kill Joe that particular night? And at that particular time? If Hector were going to rob the restaurant, he would have done it earlier in the evening. He would have stolen while there was still money in the cash register."

"That's true. But remember that Marlene was still there. She left only minutes before he did. Kominski thinks he wasn't aware that the evening's earnings had already been placed in the safe."

"Did you find out who posted Hector's bond?"

"It was Leland Johansson," said David. "He's one of the few people in town who could afford even the ten percent cost."

That's interesting, thought Shea.

"David," said Shea changing the subject, "I'm really worried about Berta. She hasn't called me today."

He frowned before he replied. "I wouldn't worry too much. She's got an elderly mother who lives alone on the south side of town. I'll bet she called Berta for something, and Berta went over there to help. You know she has to take the bus to get anywhere. And her mother doesn't have a phone. She'll call you as soon as she gets back."

Unconvinced, Shea sat in silent consideration.

"Okay, if it will make you feel any better, I will drive over there after I'm through with one thing. The chief wants me to help transport a subject to the county jail in Fort Stockton. It should take me a few hours to get there and back."

"I would really appreciate it," she said feeling guilty that she was always relying on him.

"Hasn't George returned?"

"No, he had some truck trouble. He'll be in later."

After David left, Shea walked again to the nursery to visit Mark. The next few hours passed quickly as time often does in a hospital whenever one wants rest. Shea filled out forms to obtain a social security number for Mark, she arranged for the hospital photographer to take photographs of the newborn, and she did more than the suggested exercise for a new mother.

Father Jim stopped by to give her communion and to discuss potential dates for the baptism.

"Have you chosen godparents yet?" he asked.

Shea shook her head. Jerri and Zach would be her first choices, but Jerri was Jewish and Zach was a Quaker.

"I think that Berta and George would be great, don't you?" she asked the young priest.

"Absolutely. I'll have the parish secretary call you with the times and dates for Christianing classes. You'll enjoy attending them."

When Mary brought in her dinner tray, she told Shea, "Something else has arrived for you. I'll go get it." She returned moments later with a large red-striped diaper bag wrapped in cellophane.

Shea pulled out a card which read "You can get anything online now. Isn't that great? Love, Vivian, Zach, and Jerri."

Tearing off the cellophane, Shea discovered that again there was a gift within a gift, because the bag was jammed with assorted toiletries and novelties for a newborn. Baby shampoo, lotion, soap, hooded towels and washcloths assured that the new mother could properly bathe her baby. A plastic bag held a variety of tiny tools, including a comb and brush, baby scissors, clippers, and a thermometer. She was admiring a multicolored teething toy and wondering when her baby would need such a thing when George walked into the room without bothering to knock.

"I was told you'd need one of these contraptions," he said plunking down a denim-covered baby car seat. "Otherwise they won't let me take you and the baby home in the truck."

"It's beautiful," said Shea. "Where did you get it?"

"I stopped by the Super Store on Highway 52 on the way home. Thought those dummies over in Alpine would never get the right tire, and I'd never get out of there."

"Have you talked to Berta?"

"No, the dang fool probably left the telephone off the hook. She's done that before. I'm going home now and see what she's doin'. That little pup you had is awfully tiny. He goin'to be all right?"

Assuring George that the baby would indeed be fine and that he had nothing to worry about, Shea thanked him again before he left.

"I'm going home now, child, but I'll be back in the morning. Is there anything you need before I go?" asked Mary who had passed George on his way out the door.

"Do you think I could have an aspirin or something so that I could sleep? I'm a little tired."

"Sure now. 'Tis an easy thing to do."

As David turned into Mulberry Drive, the pine tree-lined street on which the O'Daniels House stood, he was relieved to see the red Ford truck in the driveway.

At least George has returned, he thought. So everything must be all right. It had taken him longer than he had estimated to transport the criminal, wanted for domestic violence, to Fort Stockton. He went to the back door as was his custom whenever he was visiting George or Berta. Finding the screen door unlocked as usual he went inside. The first thing he saw was George sitting at the butcher block table. Strangely he didn't even look up when David entered.

"George, is something wrong? Are you feeling all right?"

"I found her right over there. I think she's dead."

Hurrying in the direction in which George was pointing, David found Berta Rivera lying on the hardwood floor in the foyer at the foot of the staircase. A flower vase with its spilled contents, water and roses, lay scattered around her. Her mouth was covered with masking tape and her hands were bound behind her. David felt for her pulse.

"She's alive, George," he shouted to the older man. At the same time, he gently pulled off the masking tape and cut the twine around her wrists with his knife. He could hear her gentle breathing. "I'm calling for an ambulance. Just stay right there."

After making calls to the hospital for an ambulance and to headquarters for help, David located a blanket upstairs to put over Berta, made sure that there was no broken glass near her body, and then returned to the kitchen.

"Why didn't you call for help?" he asked George, not unkindly.

"I don't know. I had just left the hospital, and I came right here.

When I saw her lyin' there, I just went sorta blank. I don't know how long I been here."

Leaving George still sitting at the table, David went outside to the driveway and felt the hood of the truck.

"Your engine is still warm," he told the man. "So you must have arrived just before I did."

Unwilling to touch the housekeeper since he didn't know the extent of her injuries, David made a quick tour of the house. Everywhere there was evidence that someone had been searching the home. Kitchen drawers and cabinets were open with their contents thrown on the floor or into the sink. In the parlor and living room chair and sofa cushions had been removed and tossed to the side. Upstairs the situation was the same. In each bedroom dresser drawers were open and contents flung on beds. Even Shea's desk had been thoroughly searched.

When he returned to the first floor, Aaron Kominski and Gary Armstrong had arrived. Gary was taking pictures of the crime scene.

"You guys through with her?" asked one of the ambulance drivers. "We need to get her to the hospital."

"Go ahead," said Aaron curtly without sparing a glance at the woman.

"Will she be all right?" David asked the paramedic.

"She's got a weak pulse and she's disoriented. We'll start an IV and heart monitors. Call Mesa Medical later, Officer," said the young man.

"Get pictures of all these rooms before you dust," Aaron was telling Gary. "Have you questioned the old man?"

"It's George Fallchurch," said David. "He lives in the apartment over the garage. He told me that he had just returned from Alpine. He was stuck there all night because of car trouble."

"Did you check that out?"

"Do you want me to investigate George?" asked David incredulously. "He's known Berta for years. He wouldn't do this."

"I don't know about that. An old woman just dies, leaves all her stuff to different people. I heard that her maid got some very valuable knick-knacks."

"Why would he trash the house? What was he looking for?"

"I don't know," said Kominski tensely. "Why don't you take him downtown and ask him?"

Hesitant to pursue the point any further, David went into the kitchen.

"I'm afraid I'm going to have to ask you to come downtown with

62

me and make a statement," he told George.

"I was afraid of that." George stood up slowly. He was regaining a little of his pluckiness. "This was his idea wasn't it?"

David knew to whom George was referring. Smiling, he nodded his head.

At the police station, David made a quick telephone call to the garage in Alpine where George's truck had been fixed. He also called the motel and verified that George had stayed there the previous night. Finally, he called the hospital and talked to the heavily-accented admitting doctor in the emergency room.

"Yes, Officer, this patient has been hit with a heavy object, probably glass, because there were shards in her hair," said Dr. Yadiri.

"How long ago did this happen?"

"From the discoloration and swelling of her hands and feet we can tell that she's been bound for approximately ten to twelve hours."

David breathed a sigh of relief for George, but his anxiety still wasn't lessened.
"How is she doing, Doctor?"

"She's stable, right now and resting, but she can't be questioned."

David had finished typing George's statement on the computer just as Kominski entered the room.

"Can I go now?" growled George.

"He check out?" asked Kominski of David.

"Yes, both the garage and motel verified that he was there. And Dr. Yadiri at Mesa Medical said that the attack occurred ten or twelve hours ago. It must have happened right after I talked to her last night."

Kominski sat down in a swivel chair and propped his feet up on a desk. David knew that the desk belonged to Hank Hatfield. Hank hated it when anyone touched his desk, and Kominski knew that.

"What about Hector Lopez?" he mused while toying with a picture of Hank's wife and three freckle-faced, red-haired children. He put it back on the desk face down. "He was released yesterday wasn't he?"

"Yes," said David reluctantly. He knew what was coming next.

"Call the Roadhouse and find out if he was there between the hours of 10 p.m. and 2 a.m."

David rang the restaurant, spoke for a few minutes to Ceci De Anda, and turned back to Kominski.

"He was not at the restaurant during that shift. He came in early this morning to work. He's still there."

"Pick him up," ordered Kominski and headed for his office. "I'm going to the hospital to question that maid. She knows something."

"I'll go with you, David," said Gary who had just returned from the O'Daniels house. "This is not going to be pleasant."

"No, kidding."

At the restaurant Gary and David noticed that the parking lot was packed. This was normal for a Saturday evening, but there was probably a bit of morbid curiosity on the part of a few people who wanted to view the scene of the murder. Inside the restaurant Ceci tensed when she saw the two policemen enter the building. Before she could say anything, Hector Lopez peered through the small window which separated the kitchen from the counter area. In another second, he had thrown down his utensil and was sprinting for the door.

"Stop, Hector," shouted both David and Gary in unison.

Both men raced after the slender and surprisingly agile young cook. As startled customers pushed back their chairs to allow the patrolmen to pass, several others looked as if they wanted to join in the chase. David, thirty pounds lighter than Gary and an ex-track athlete, made it first to the back exit. Outside he saw Hector leaping on an old motorcycle and gunning the starter. Choosing not to draw his revolver or make idle threats, Kyle took a running leap and threw himself at the suspect. Both men tumbled to the ground and rolled over. Jumping to his feet, Hector swung a fist at David and connected with his chin.

"Enough, Hector," said David. He slammed the young man against a parked car, presumably Ceci's, turned him around, bent his head over the hood, and pinned his arms back so that Gary could handcuff him. "That was a really stupid thing to do."

"I heard about Berta, ese. She's in the hospital now. And of course you guys think I did it? Why would I go to that house? I've never been there before."

"Don't have a clue fella," said Gary as they led Hector to the patrolcar, pushed his head down, and put him in the back seat. "Not a clue."

"Running away isn't going to help things, Hector," said David. He held no ill will against the man for hitting him. Hell, if he had been in the same situation, he might have done worse. "You'll need to call your lawyer as soon as we get to the station."

After Hector was booked, he was led into a room where he

called Jessica Gutierrez. David sat down with Gary to write up the report.

"What do we know?" he asked his partner. "Someone is looking for something, that's for sure. Is that why Dorothy was killed, and her purse was stolen? What does this guy want? What is it that he thinks Dorothy has?"

At that moment Kominski strode into the room. "Looks like you got it pretty bad," he smirked. "How does the other guy look?"

"It wasn't a big deal," said David.

"Sure it is," said Kominski. "We can add assaulting an officer to his list of offenses. And resisting arrest. If that doesn't add up to a confession of guilt, I don't know what does."

"What did Berta tell you?" asked David.

"She said she didn't see who hit her. She couldn't give me any more details than that foreign doctor. Now why do you think all the doctors are foreigners these days? What's this guy, an Arab or Indian or something?" said Kominski.

"I don't know, Sergeant. Why are all investigators Polish?" retorted Gary.

"I'm Russian," sneered the investigator and walked toward the interrogation room where Hector was waiting. "I'm going to question Lopez again. Oh, by the way, De Vargas. That maid wanted to talk to you. Said that it had to be you."

"I'll go over right now," said De Vargas, grabbing his hat.

"Do you think you might need some help?" asked Gary. David looked at him in surprise. "I mean, do you think that new doctor, that Dr. MacKenzie, might be around?"

"She's a pediatrician, Gary," said David with a smile. "She would be in the nursery if she's there. Do you think we should interrogate some of the newborns?"

"Maybe not." Gary grinned at David. "But you gotta give a guy credit for trying. She really is a looker."

"And maybe she read that personal ad that was in the newspaper and wants to meet 'an African-American male who loves jazz'."

"Yeah, real funny. I'm going to kill that Hank Hatfield one of these days."

Hank Hatfield, a church-going father of three who had been married for eighteen years, was the practical joker in the department. He had almost split his sides with laughter when he saw Gary's horrified expression as he read the fake ad.

"Well, I'm going back to the O'Daniels house to see if Jaime needs any help," said David, "and make sure that everything is secure."

Jaime Chavez and almost every available patrolman had been called in for extra duty. Gary waved at the night dispatcher. "I'll check in later, Helen."

"You boys take care," she said as she did every night. "And give Berta my love, David. Oh, and could you stop by and give this to Shea for her baby." She handed him a gift bag decorated with pink and blue storks. "I hand-knitted these booties and this sweater myself."

At the hospital David was told that Shea was still asleep and would probably rest all night. He left the gift bag with the night nurse, and went to the Intensive Care Unit. Dr. Yadiri, who did indeed look like he hailed from India, said that he would allow David five minutes with Berta.

"That other officer upset her very much. I thought he was rather rude," said the soft-spoken physician.

"I won't take much time," promised David. He walked softly into the room. Berta was hooked up to several monitors and had a nasty bruise on her face where she hit it on the floor.

"Hi, Berta. Feeling any better?"

"David," she said. "I've been asleep."

"Detective Kominski said that you didn't get a look at whoever hit you," said David. "Did you remember something after you talked to him?"

"No, I told him everything. I don't know if it was a man or a woman. I really don't know anything else. But I wanted to tell you something."

"What is it, Berta?" David had to lean over to hear her voice which had sunk to a whisper.

"I think that Shea is in danger, David. Don't let her go back to that house."

Mesa Medical Chile Verde

1 1/2 lb boneless beef
chopped into 1 inch cubes
2 12-ounce cans tomatoes
1/3 cup chopped parsley
1/2 t sugar
1 large can chopped green chiles

3 Tb vegetable oil
1 green bell
pepper, diced
1 minced garlic
1 cup water
Salt

1. Brown meat in frying pan. Set aside.
2. Saute bell pepper and garlic with oil until soft.
3. In large saucepan mix tomatoes, chiles, parsley, salt, water. Bring to a boil.
4. Reduce heat to simmer. Add meat and sauteed vegetables.
5. Cover and simmer for two hours, stirring occasionally.
6. Remove cover, simmer another 45 minutes until sauce is thick.

Sports News

The Cedars Apartment soccer team, in the 12 to 14-year-old league, played the Mesa Trailer Park soccer team on Saturday. The "Trailer Parkers" beat the "Cedar Spruces" 6-0 and are unde-feated for the season.

The "Over Sixty Swim Club" practices at the City Pool on Thursday afternoons. Everyone is urged to wear protection and toggles.

City Council has appropriated $500 to the City Parks to organize coed softball teams. Volunteer coaches are needed.

(Editor's Note: Saturday's obituary should have read "Mrs. O'Daniels *is survived by* her granddaughters.")

CHAPTER FIVE

The next morning Shea awoke with a headache. Even in her dreams she worried about finances, it seemed. During the night she dreamt that she was homeless, sitting on a busy city curb with a ragged bundle in her arms. Kind of a maternal Eliza Doolittle, she thought wryly.

Well, it's not quite that bad, she told herself. Mark and I have the house rent-free, and in the fall Antonio Gonzalez, History department chair at Mesa State University, has promised me two adjunct-lecturer classes. Each American history course paid two thousand dollars which would be a big help.

Using a legal pad she carried in her backpack, Shea began to scribble mathematical figures. On the credit side, she had her own savings plus what was left by her grandmother. At present it totaled a little under $5,000. On the debit side, she calculated estimates for monthly food, gas, electricity, water, and telephone bills. She included necessities for the car, such as gas, oil, and monthly insurance. She added another figure for unexpected expenses, such as car or appliance repairs.

What was really bothering her were the medical expenses. Dr. MacKenzie, who insisted that Shea call her Vanessa, had told Shea yesterday that Mark would be in the hospital for at least a week, perhaps more. Although her university expenses would cover the majority of the cost, Shea had to cover the co-payment. At this rate the hospital and doctors' bills were going to take a huge chunk out of her checking account.

Speaking of which, she thought, I will have to open one tomorrow. I still haven't gotten around to it. She firmly resolved that when Dr. Martin walked through the door, she would accost him about early release. It had been thirty-two hours since she gave birth, Shea noted, glancing at her wristwatch on the side table.

When the door pushed open, it wasn't Dr. Martin who entered. Instead George, his face lined with worry, stomped over to her bed.

"George, I didn't expect you back so soon."

"I got some bad news kiddo."

"More car trouble?" asked Shea. It would be a shame if George had inherited a lemon. He really needed a new truck.

"Nah. Much worse. Someone broke into your grandmother's house yesterday and knocked out poor Berta."

"What? Where is she? I've got to see her." Feeling guilty that while she had been alternately basking in the glow of her newborn or fretting over money, Berta was lying somewhere in pain, Shea threw off her covers. "I'm going to see her, where is she?"

"Just calm down a minute," barked George. "Here's yer breakfast. Have some coffee. That always calms ya down. She's been moved to a room on the second floor. I just been there, and she's asleep."

George brought a styrofoam cup to Shea from the tray which had just been left by a girl in a candy-striped uniform, one of the hospital's teen-aged volunteers.

"Tell me what happened," said Shea, a little more meekly as she sipped the hot brew. Not like hers, but not bad.

"It seems that right after David called her and told her about the baby that it happened. Someone was in the house and came right up behind her, bonked her on the head, and knocked her clean out. Sorry kiddo, but whoever it was done broke that expensive vase of your great-grandma's, you know the one she ordered from Ireland."

Shea nodded. It was her great grandmother Isabel who had added to the family furnishings by purchasing a complete set of Waterford crystal, from various goblets to flower vases to the chandeliers that hung in the foyer and over the dining table. Everything had been sent from Ireland, arriving without a single crack. In addition the same ancestor had ordered expensive Irish linen for the dining room and bedrooms.

I might be almost broke, thought Shea, but I'm certainly broke with style.

"After they knocked her out, they tied her up and put some tape over her mouth," continued George. He paused when he saw Shea grimace. "She's doin' okay, kiddo. That's what that Dr. Yadiri says. Fellow talks funny, but he knows his stuff."

"Do they have any idea who did this or why?" asked Shea.

"Nope. Nothin' was taken, just a lot of stuff thrown around. David took me down to the station, asked me a lot of questions. Then he called up that garage and motel in Alpine. They vouched for me. So I'm off th' hook."

George beamed at Shea, obviously a little proud that at least for a short while he had been a criminal suspect.

70

"David De Vargas did what?"

George looked perturbed at her tone, which was angrier than he had ever heard.

"He had no right to even question you! Wait until I see him. I'll give him a piece of my mind."

"Now you won't do any such thing, girl. He was just doin' his job. That's what a policeman does."

Shea's fuming was interrupted when Dr. John Martin walked into the room. His presence always lowered the anxiety level around him by at least ten to twenty percent. A contemporary of George's and Dorothy's, he was well over six feet, white-haired and perpetually calm under any circumstances. John Martin should have retired ten years go, but too many of his patients said that they simply wouldn't have their babies without him. Since some of these women were already fully dilated, it seemed sensible to remain in practice.

"Hullo, John. Didn't know you were still alive."

"How are you, George? Didn't know they let you out of the house anymore."

While the two old classmates bantered, Shea submitted to Dr. Martin's ministrations which included an examinatin with his stethoscope and some uncomfortable probing of her stomach.

"I'm not going to do another vaginal examination," said Dr. Martin to the supreme relief of George, a long-confirmed bachelor and committed avoider of anything pertaining to female issues. George looked like he was about to bolt for Oklahoma. "You seem to be recovering just fine."

That statement gave Shea the opening that she needed. "Dr. Martin do you think I can be released this morning? I know you like to keep your patients longer, but, well, the baby's going to be here anyway, and I can't, well I just can't . . ."

"Afford it?" finished the doctor for her. "I'll do this on the condition that if you have any discomfort or any pain that you come immediately to my office. And I would really like for you to stay with someone. Have you thought of that?"

"You can't go back to the house for a couple of days, Shea," said George. "It's a crime scene now, and the police don't want nothin' touched."

"I'll think of something," said Shea.

"You can stay in my apartment," offered George, but Shea just shook her head. George's apartment was too small, and it smelled of fish bait. Besides he would go crazy if he had a woman, even someone of whom he was genuinely fond, around for more than fifteen minutes.

When the two men left, Shea showered and dressed in the knit pants and top which she had worn upon her arrival. The clothes now hung dangerously loose on her, and she wondered if she would be allowed to enter the house long enough to collect a few clothes. She didn't think she was ready for jeans yet, but she thought she could fit into her sundresses and pre-maternity elastic-waist shorts.

Having blow-dried her straight hair until it hung smooth, Shea emerged from the bathroom, dressed for the day. Right now her hair was just inches above her shoulders, and she was considering whether or not to grow it longer or cut it short. Dismissing the decision as something that could wait for awhile, she walked down the hallway to make her morning visit to the nursery. Although she wasn't offered the option of breast-feeding the baby, since he was premature and underweight, she was allowed to hold him and give him a bottle. It was the best part of her day.

"Just the young lady I wanted to see," said a booming voice.

Coming toward Shea was Sheriff Beau Cummings. A couple of inches shy of six feet, the Chief sported a ruddy complexion and a prominent beer belly. He also had the best western twang in the county and was usually chewing gum which prevented him from indulging in his other favorite pastime, chomping on a cigar. Beau usually reserved that vice for fishing or deer hunting.

In almost every respect save two things Beau Cummings represented the image of a good old boy, a Texas native, and the quintessential country peace officer. The first exception was that Chief Cummings was uncommonly shrewd when it came to crime and vice. He had seen quite a bit of both in his forty years as a small-town policeman, and he usually got to the bottom of matters. The second exception was another unstereotypical characteristic. Unlike the corrupt, inept Hollywood version of a backwoods police chief, Cummings was sincerely devoted to the welfare of his Mesa citizens. Whenever someone was harmed, as in the case of Berta Rivera, or murdered, as in the case of Dorothy O'Daniels, he took it personally.

Cummings had vowed to solve this case if it took every police officer on the force working double shifts until he had the answers. Because he still wasn't convinced that Hector Lopez had committed either he murder or the attack, he had sent police officers to interview each guest who had attended the funeral reception at the O'Daniels home. They needed more clues. No matter how long Aaron Kominski hammered at Hector, the young cook wouldn't break and confess.

There was simply no motive, no rhyme or reason for these crimes, thought Beau. All we have is some circumstantial evidence. Not enough, he said to himself, as hestopped in front of the new mother.

"How are you doing, Shea?"

"I'm just fine, Chief." Although she always referred to her lawyer as Mr. Tyler and her obstetrician as Dr. Martin, the head of the police department was known to everyone in town as either Beau or Chief. "I'm going to feed my new son and then visit Berta. What can you tell me about what happened?"

"Still a bunch of dead ends. Berta didn't see anything before she was hit with that vase. The house was trashed, but nothing else was really damaged. And unfortunately whoever did this came well prepared. They wore gloves."

"So there are no fingerprints?"

"Not a one. Shea," said Cummings, lowering his voice and pulling the girl off to the side of the corridor. "Whoever did this knew the house fairly well. We think they had been in there before. We also think the intruder was looking for something specific. What is it that your grandmother could have had on her person or in the house that could make someone commit a murder?"

"I honestly don't know. There are a few nice pieces of jewelry, some pearls and maybe a pair of diamond earrings, but that's all. And I believe those are in a safe deposit box at the bank."

"I've got my men out talking to people who attended the reception. If you think of anything, you'll call me, right?"

"Yes, Chief."

The portly police chief left her and made his way down the hallway, hailing people right and left. He was exceptionally popular and universally respected. Even more important, he made the population feel safe.

Inside the nursery Shea put on the gown and face mask which was still required for contact with the baby. The intensive care nurse put Mark in her arms, and she crooned softly to him while she gave him a couple of ounces of formula.

He's so vulnerable, she thought. He seems too precarious to even breathe.

All too soon the nurse took him from her to replace the infant in the oxygen tent.

On her way from the room, Shea ran into Dr. MacKenzie.

"Shea, I'm glad I caught you," said the doctor.

Shea looked at her admiringly, wondering how the doctor, with

73

her late-night deliveries and early morning rounds managed to look so fresh and fetching. Vanessa's jet-black hair was pulled back in a bun, emphasizing her high cheek bones and almond-shaped eyes. The white lab coat she wore over an emerald dress contrasted nicely with her creamy brown skin.

"How is Mark doing?" Shea asked.

"He's doing better, but he will need some special care when he leaves here. For example, he will need to be on oxygen twenty-four hours a day. He'll require some respiratory equipment and a few medications. And he will need round-the-clock care. Not necessarily a nurse, but someone who has been trained in hospital care."

Shea listened with a sinking feeling. Every bit of news was worse than the last. How could she afford such expensive treatment?

"His lungs are improving, but this process takes months. Do you have anyone that could come and help you?"

Shea tried to imagine her mother or her sister nursing an infant around the clock. The image was ludicrous. Berta was incapacitated right now, and of course, George was out of the question. Her friends all had jobs and their own responsibilities. She shook her head.

"Shea, I know you don't want to do this, but I think you need to apply for county assistance," said Vanessa softly so that no one else could hear.

"Vanessa, let me think about it."

As tactful as her father, the doctor chose not to press the issue at the moment. Shea was walking toward the elevator to take to the second floor when she was confronted by Mary O'Malley who had just come on duty.

"I brought you a bit of a treat," she said, handing Shea a plastic container. When
Shea opened the lid, she encountered a wonderful smell. "It's me own special quiche. I thought you'd be good and tired of this hospital food."

"You're right," said Shea.

"Why so glum, me darling?"

"Well, for starters I can't even return to my own house. Now that I have a house. You heard what happened to Berta Rivera?"

"No, I just got here. Tell me."

Elevators came and went while Shea related the attack on Berta, the police cordoning off the house, and her own homeless predicament. She concluded with Dr. MacKenzie's recent relevations concerning a live-in health care provider.

"So not only do I have no place to live, I also need to hire around-the-clock help," complained Shea. She knew that she was whining, but after all, she felt she was entitled.

Mary O'Malley had stood, listening patiently with several folders in her hands. "I need to deliver these forms to the nurse's station on the fourth floor," she said, "but I'll come to your room in a bit. You'll be checking out this morning?"

"Yes, I'm going to visit Berta and then wait for the release papers."

"I'll be right back."

Feeling oddly relieved now that she had vented all her emotions, Shea made her way to Berta's room where she spent a few minutes. This time she did the consoling while Berta, through a sea of tears, apologized for not being able to help Shea when she would bring home her son.

"I meant to be there, Shea. But mi madre got very scared when I was hit. She wants to take a vacation in Mexico and visit all our relatives in Guanajuato. She wants to leave as soon as I get out of the hospital. I just can't tell her no."

"Berta, I understand, and I don't blame you in the least," said Shea soothingly. Actually she wanted to know if she could jump on the bus with them.

"At least Marlene will be around to help you," said Berta.

"Marlene is out of town. Apparently she went fishing with Bob Crockett."

"That Bob from the restaurant?" said Berta. "He has a cabin up in Silver Lake. I never knew Marlene to go there before."

"Well, hopefully we will hear from them soon."

As Shea left the room, she thought about Berta's final comment. Were Bob and Marlene in Silver Lake? If not, then where were they?

"Am I the only one in town who didn't go to this dang funeral reception?" groused Hank Hatfield. He and David were sitting in the station, determining who was left to interview. Gary Armstrong had already gone to the hospital after practically arm-wrestling each man for the privilege of questioning Dr. MacKenzie. He had left with a big smile on his face.

"We've already gone through quite a few. There's still the girls at the Mesa Roadhouse. You know the two sisters," said David.

"And Leland Johannson."

"I can't stand that prissy son-of-a-bitch," said Hank. "I'll take Edna Grunderson, Ralph Atteberry out on Country Club Road, and Manuel Escudero. His farm is right next to the Atteberry place."

"Did anybody interview Father Jim or Jason Tyler?"

"Kominski wanted to do that himself. I guess he's safe with a priest and a lawyer. They probably won't shoot him when he insults them."

David smiled at the use of the word "when" instead of "if." It was a foregone conclusion. "What about Bob Crockett?"

"Beau called the state park rangers up at Silver Lake. You know that itty-bitty operation. This would be in their jurisdiction. Well, they agreed to go out to Bob's cabin and tell him he was needed back here, but there was no one in the cabin. His SUV was there and so was his boat. Sometimes Bob likes to take his camping gear and backpack into the wilds. You might not see him for days."

"With Marlene?" asked David. He pictured Marlene with her perfectly coiffed hair and expertly manicured nails. Backpacking was not an image he associated with her.

"You never know," said Hank with all the experience of a long-suffering husband. "A woman will do a lot of things to land a man."

"I hope he shows up soon," said David.

"I do too. What with Hector locked up and Bob missing, we ain't never going to get another decent meal at the Roadhouse."

"I hear that Hester Fernshaw is filling in as cook."

"Damn, that woman overcooks everything. She could burn a salad."

They both left to do their respective interviews. At the Mesa Roadhouse, David found Ceci taking her shift while Rosie remained at home with their mother.

"No, David, I can't remember anything unusual happening. People were just standing around, being kind of serious. You know how subdued they are after a funeral. I didn't notice anything unusual."

"Were people milling around a lot? Looking at things?"

Ceci looked a little embarrassed. "Well, Rosie and I had to go upstairs to use the bathroom. And we kind of peeked into some of the bedrooms. We'd never been inside the O'Daniels house before, and we were, you know, curious."

David smiled. Ceci was such a well-behaved young woman that even the thought of a little harmless snooping was a high crime and misdemeanor for her.

"Did you see anyone else 'peeking' around the house?"

"No, but Berta did get awfully mad at Bob. He had gone into the kitchen to get a knife to cut some meat or something. You know how he likes to take charge. And Berta practically ran him off with a rolling pin."

This time David had to stifle a chuckle. The thought of petite, plump Berta chasing off burly, ham-fisted Bob was something out of a Looneytoons cartoon.

"What did you and Rosie do when you left the reception?"

"I came home and changed. I had to take the night shift, which I don't like at all. But since we're so short-handed at the restaurant, Rosie and I have been taking turns."

"How long were you here?" David tried to make the question sound casual, but Ceci didn't seem to notice anything unusual.

"Until two o'clock. Hester Fernshaw is filling in as cook for the boys. Her son, Curtis, is dishwasher and bus boy. We have an agreement now that no one should be left alone in the restaurant so we three left together."

Kyle's next stop was the De Anda home. The small prairie-style home was only a few blocks from Pinon Lane in an old, but well-kept and quiet neighborhood. Most of the residents were retired and elderly.

It must be a pretty boring place for a couple of young girls, he thought. Even if they are dependable and stable like Ceci and Rosie. When he rang the doorbell, it took a couple of minutes for Rosie to emerge from the second floor and answer the door.

"Hi, David," she said, obviously pleased to have a visitor. "Come in."

David followed her into the living room. He couldn't help but notice that although the place was spotlessly clean, the furniture was showing a lot of wear and tear. The flowered cushions on the sofa and wing chairs were faded and torn in some spots, and the television set was at least a ten-year-old model. Paint was chipping off the walls in certain spots. There was a faint smell of must and mildew as if the windows weren't often opened to let the house air. And the place was uncommonly quiet. This was definitely the home of a sick person.

"How is your mother doing?" asked David. Since he had a perfectly healthy mother, who had remarried after his father's death and moved to Austin, he couldn't imagine taking care of a sick parent. Especially at such a young age.

"She has her good and her bad days," sighed Rosie. "Today is not such a good day. She's in some pain."

"Do you have to sedate her sometimes for the pain?" asked Kyle.

"Sometimes. We try not to do that, but it can get unbearable for her."

David then proceeded to ask Rosie the same questions he had asked Ceci. The only time they differed in their answers was in their activities after the reception.

"Ceci had to take the night shift, so I came home to be with Mother."

"Do you remember what time you went to bed?"

She paused a moment as if considering. "Sometime around ten o'clock. I set the alarm for two in the morning so that I could give Mother her medications."

"Did anyone call you or did you call anyone during that time period?"

Rosie, a little more cautious than her unsuspecting sister, looked David straight in the eye. "No. I didn't talk to anyone. The only one who was here was my mother. And she was asleep."

David left the De Anda house with a bad taste in his mouth. He really hated questioning people who were his friends and whom he had known his whole life. That didn't necessarily include Leland Johannson, who was his next stop. Although Leland was another long-time resident of Mesa, he had never been the friendliest of residents. He had made pretty good money in his lifetime with his restaurant, feed and grain store, and market. Unlike the O'Daniels who came from old money and old stock, Johannson was the son of a truck driver. Through sheer determination, street smarts, and marrying the owner's daughter, Katie Svenson, Johannson had worked his way up in the local grocery store from stock boy to owner. During some bad times and recessions which had hit the town hard, he had bought out the feed and grain and the restaurant, renamed them, and turned them into profitable businesses.

In his personal life, Johannson was not nearly as successful. He had divorced and remarried three times, and his exes lived in other states with his various offspring. Although Texas law did not allow for alimony, it certainly provided for generous child support payments. David had heard rumors that Johannson's child support bills were taking him to the cleaners, so to speak. He had also heard that Johannson's various enterprises had experienced a couple of bad years recently, as all businesses do occasionally.

David had been surprised to see Leland at the funeral reception. He seldom went to town functions, preferring to spend his time golfing at the Alpine Country Club or flying off to Dallas to catch a Texas Rangers game. Dorothy, however, was special. Perhaps that was why Leland made an exception.

Taking Highway 52 again, David drove north in the opposite direction of the Roadhouse. He knew he would find Leland Johannson in his office in the grain and feed as usual. Johannson liked to run all of his businesses from this spot, possibly, thought David, because it was in the most remote location, and he had to deal with less people.

Pulling into the unpaved parking lot, David saw Manuel Escudero carrying what looked like a thirty-pound sack of chicken feed to his truck. Manuel had at least twenty-five years on the policeman, but he still put in a sixteen hour day on his farm.

"Hey, David," said Manuel. "Que pasa?"

"No pasa nada."

"Your buddy Hank Hatfield came out to talk to me and Ralph Attebury. Ralph got pretty riled up at being asked some personal questions. But I said, Ralph, just shut up and answer the man. You know that both of us were in bed with our wives at that hour, and we don't got nothing to hide. How's Berta doing?"

"She's going to be okay."

David left the man to his work and walked into the feed and grain. At this rate, they would have the whole town pissed off at the police department by supper time. He walked past various shoppers, mostly farmers in denim coveralls or ranchers in sturdy cowboy hats and boots, who stared at him with undisguised curiosity. By now everyone knew that the police were interviewing anyone who had been at the reception. A few of them privately wished that they had attended just to be in on the excitement.

"Damnation," muttered one man to a friend, "my only chance to be a suspect in a crime, and I decided to mow the lawn instead."

Pausing to knock on the window of the door, David walked in as Leland waved at him from his desk.

"What can I do for you, Officer?" he asked politely.

David had not a doubt that Johannson knew why he was in his office, but he decided to play the game. "We're questioning everyone, Mr. Johannson, who was at Dorothy O'Daniels' funeral reception. We're trying to find any leads as to why Berta Rivera was attacked later that night."

"And perhaps find some leads concerning the murder of Dorothy O'Daniels?"

David suppressed a feeling of impatience, but he couldn't let Johannson goad him.

"The two events certainly may be related," he said, choosing his words carefully.

"Could you tell me what happened at the reception?"

"I spent a great deal of time comforting the granddaughter of Mrs. O'Daniels," said Johannson. "She was very distraught. As you know, Dorothy was very dear to me. She had worked at the restaurant long before I bought it. Not only was she a valued employee, but she was a fine woman."

"Did you talk to anyone else or notice anything unusual?"

"No, as I said, I talked mostly to Megan O'Daniels."

I just bet you did, thought David. "What did you do when you left the reception?"

"I came here. I had some paperwork to do. You know with three businesses there are always bills to pay and accounts to balance." He gave David a small, tight smile.

"How long did you remain here?"

"Until almost one o'clock. And if your next question is, was anyone with me, the answer is no. And no, I didn't talk to anyone while I was here. No, I don't have an alibi. And no, I didn't go back to the O'Daniels' house and smash Berta Rivera's head with a vase. I would have no reason to do so. That would be very bad for business."

Walking back to his police cruiser, David thought, Hank is right. This guy really is a prissy son-of-a-bitch. When he arrived back at the station house, it didn't help his attitude to see Gary Armstrong grinning broadly while he typed up his report.

"I had a really nice interview with Dr. MacKenzie," he said as if David couldn't have guessed.

"Did you really?" David was in no mood to hear about it.

"Yeah. She is one fine lady. Hey, do you think she would go out with me?"

"I don't know. I'll ask her during study hall."

Mary O'Malley caught up again with Shea in the intensive care nursery where Shea was having her third visit of the day. She had been processed and had gone to the business office to pay her portion of the hospital bill. It wasn't too bad. While she was there, however, she had asked them to estimate what they thought the baby's stay would cost. The figure had sent her head spinning.

"So, wouldn't you know I have an offer to make," said Mary. Shea had learned that her lilting Irish accent usually conveyed a no-nonsense message. "You have no place to stay for a few days, and I have such a place. I've got meself one of those cute apartments over in 'The Cedars', a one bedroom."

Shea knew the place. It was a new apartment complex, renting mostly to young singles or to older people who had just sold their homes. A lot of college students, the out-of-towners, stayed there.

"It's not far from the hospital. And you could stay a couple of days to keep me company. You know I don't know a soul in this town yet except for the people in the hospital."

"That would be nice," said Shea. "But I wouldn't want to impose."

"That you wouldn't be doing," said Mary firmly. "You and I could come to the hospital each day so that you can be with your wee boy. Then maybe in the evening we could watch a bit of telly."

When Shea hesitated, Mary continued. "Actually I have an ulterior motive. I really don't like staying in those apartments. You know how they are, they're the ones that have the swimming pool and club house. Lots of young people walking around with their dogs or cooking out of doors."

Shea nodded. She vaguely recalled that someone had said David De Vargas had an efficiency apartment there. She wondered what it was like to feel young and carefree enough to hang around a swimming pool or a club house.

"And I know that you live in that grand house on Mulberry Lane," Mary continued. "Or is it Pinon?" Instead of pronouncing it 'pin-yon', Mary said 'pine on.' "Anyway, I was thinking that what with paying for rent and utilities and having to run to the laundry to wash me clothes, I could be giving you that money and staying in one of your extra rooms. Then you wouldn't have to be alone when you return to that big place. And I could help you with little Mark when I'm not here at the hospital."

Shea looked at her in wonder. Actually that wasn't a bad idea. Sort of like having a paying house guest, she thought. It would be good to have someone else knocking around. She hadn't realized that she had felt so skittish about returning to the house until now.

"Let's give it a go," she said, using one of Mary's phrases.

Which was why at half past ten that evening, Shea was unwinding by wandering around 'The Cedars.' The complex certainly lived up to its name, thought Shea, with its wood-frame three-story apartments, tall cedar trees forming small woody areas, and pansies growing in wooden planters lining the cobblestone pathways. It was that time when the evening air was clear of the heat and dust that pervaded the earlier part of the day. As the environment shed its daily heavy exterior, Mesa residents like to relax in the soft and soothing breezes by taking late evening walks. Several people, mostly in pairs, were doing the exact same thing as herself.

"How are you tonight?"

Shea's calm was interrupted by the sound of David De Vargas' voice. He was dressed in his patrolman's uniform and carrying his hat. She assumed he must be leaving for his night shift.

"I'm fine."

"Are you staying here?" David looked perplexed.

"I'm staying with Mary O'Malley. She's a nurse's aide at the hospital. You know that I can't return to the house just yet."

"Where does she live?"

Shea pointed to the second floor about fifty yards from where they were standing.

"Believe it or not I'm just above you on the third floor. I have one of those one-room apartments."

Suddenly realized that she was consorting with the enemy, Shea remembered that she was supposed to be angry with David. "Why did you question George? Was that really necessary?"

David looked down at the hat he was carrying before he answered. "We're questioning everyone, Shea. One woman has been killed and another one attacked. And we still don't know who did this or why."

"I know," she said, catching him by surprise by agreeing with him. "It must be hard on all of you, interviewing people you've known forever. How do you do it?"

"You just do it," he shrugged. "Good night."

Watching him walk away, Shea thought he seemed more than downcast tonight. He seemed lonely. That was a feeling with which she could empathize, she thought. She missed Mark more than ever. If he had been here, his scientific mind would have analyzed the situation, sorted through facts, and he would have arrived at a workable assumption by now. And he would have done something to lift her spirits, such as telling her fake stories about the constellations in place of their real mythological origins.

"Shea, you have a telephone call."

Shea had left Mary's telephone number with the hospital in case anyone should need to be in touch. She walked slowly up the stairs, still feeling a little sore, to take the phone from Mary.

"Hello."

"Hello, darling, this is your mother."

"Where are you calling from?"

82

"We're still in Hawaii. It's heavenly here. We really needed to relax after that horrible funeral. How are you doing?"

Just fine, Mom, thought Shea wryly. I just had a baby, had a friend attacked, and I'm heading to the poor house.

"Just fine, Mom," she said.

"I was so thrilled to hear about the baby. Is he doing all right?"

"Yes, he'll be in intensive care a while longer. He was born six weeks premature."

"Well, you know they always say that any baby born past seven months will be just fine. By the way, I finally remember where I saw that woman, what was her name, Marlene."

"Where was that, Mom?"

"In Las Vegas, just as I had thought. She was losing a lot of money at the roulette wheel."

Her mother went to Las Vegas quite a lot, thought Shea. It could have been months or even years ago. "When was this?"

"Not long ago, dear. Maybe three or four weeks."

Shea listened to her mother gush about the sights they had seen in Hawaii for a few more minutes. When she hung up the telephone, she sat in silence for a moment. Marlene was in Las Vegas only a month ago, thought Shea. And she had accrued some big gambling debts. Why hadn't she said anything about that?

Come to think of it, where was Marlene?

Mary O'Malley's Quiche

1 9-inch unbaked pastry shell	1/4 c chopped onion
8 ounches shredded cheddar cheese	1 Tb flour
6 slices cooked bacon	2 Tb butter or margarine
3 eggs	1/2 t salt
1 3/4 c milk	1 long green chile, diced

1. Bake pastry shell at 450 degrees for 5 to 7 minutes.
2. Saute onion and chile in margarine or butter until tender. Stir in flour and salt.
3. In mixing bowl beat eggs and milk. Add vegetables and chopped bacon.
4. Sprinkle cheese over pastry shell. Add mixture.
5. Bake at 325 degrees for 45 minutes. Let stand 10 minutes.

La Mesa Noticia, Monday, June 10

Police Blotter

Ms. Berta Rivera was found unconscious in the home of the late Ms. Dorothy O'Daniels last Friday night. Anyone with information concerning this incident should contact the Mesa Police Department.

Manuel Escudero reported his truck was missing on Wednesday afternoon. On Thursday morning Octavia Escudero called the police to report that she had left it at a neighbor's house.

Ms. Mabel Harding, 80, was rushed to the hospital late Thursday night complaining of stomach pains. She told hospital personnel that she had taken acid and coke earlier that day.

(Editor's Note: Sunday's Sport News about the "Over Sixty Swim Club" should have read "everyone is urged to wear *UV* protection and *goggles*.")

CHAPTER SIX

It had been an especially busy day for Shea, hampered by the fact that Dr. Martin wouldn't let her drive just yet. She began early in the morning by riding to the hospital with Mary in her used station wagon. Used was an understatement. It should have qualified as an antique, Mary told her. Only no one was going to give her antique prices for that heap of junk.

After spending some time with Mark, Shea had been offered a ride to the downtown bank by Vanessa MacKenzie who was leaving to do her office hours. She and several other doctors kept offices in a pueblo-style building adjacent to the bank.

"If you don't mind my asking," said Vanessa as she turned into First Street where the bank was located, "how long were you and your husband married?"

"A little over five years." It seemed liked an incredibly short time to Shea.

"I was married too. While I was in medical school. To another med student. For about five minutes."

"What happened?" Shea couldn't help asking. "Career conflicts?"

"Female conflicts is more like it," said Vanessa with a lift of her eyebrows. "He just couldn't get enough of them."

At First City Bank, Shea opened a checking account and received some temporary checks. She shook her head when the account officer asked if she would also like to open a savings account. Handing over the documents furnished by Jason Tyler, which would effect the transfer of her grandmother's funds to her own, she then walked to the door.

"Do you need a ride somewhere?" asked Ceci De Anda who had just finished cashing a check.

"Actually I would really appreciate a ride. I need to get back to the hospital for the noon feeding."

On the way to the hospital, Shea asked the younger girl about her life in Mesa.

"Oh, we go to the movies a lot, or at least whenever we can get

85

a sitter. There's not much else to do here in Mesa. Rosie goes to the church dances, but I like to go over to Hudson's Tavern on the Interstate. They do line dancing there."

They passed over a dry riverbed which Shea remembered from her summer vacations had been a hot spot for teenage parties. She had gone only once with a friend, and they had decided to leave fairly early. They had never returned.

"Do people still get together at the river levee?" she asked.

"Yeah, sometimes. I like to go when I can get away. It's nothing wild. There's no rough stuff or drugs. Just a lot of kids with some beer and music. Rosie doesn't like it when I go. She thinks it's a bad crowd."

Shea knew from her limited experience with college parties that these gatherings were anything but innocent. There were always some drugs on hand if one wanted them, and there was also a certain amount of binge drinking. That was why she had spent most of her undergraduate days practically as a recluse. When she finally met Mark during her first week in graduate school, he had seemed like a lifeline.

Glancing sideways at Ceci and trying not to be too obvious, Shea decided that Ceci would be exceptionally pretty if she smiled more, as she was doing today, and if she wore contact lenses, rather than those black-rimmed glasses. As for herself, she wore glasses for reading purposes only, which Mark had sworn up and down was very sexy. Like most women, she refused to believe him.

At the hospital, she thanked Ceci and went again to the Intensive Care Nursery. By now she knew most of the nurses and nurse's aides, and she enjoyed sharing their daily gossip and jokes.

"Shea, you had a telephone call from a man named George," said Mary as she passed by with an armload of linens. "He said for you to call him at the house."

"George, what's up?" asked Shea who had called as soon as she had returned Mark to the bassinette.

"That investigator fellow, Komski, Komrade..."

"Do you mean Kominski?"

"Yeah, him. He gave you the green light to come and get some duds. He says
you can move back to the house in another day."

"That's good news. Would you be able to pick me up at the hospital?"

"On my way."

An hour later, Shea was in her bedroom packing a few clothes. Her breasts were still swollen and tender from the milk which she was unable to use, and she wondered what she could wear that would make her feel comfortable. She finally settled on a white cotton tee and pair of black plaid pull-on walking shorts. After choosing a couple of more outfits, she told George she was ready.

The house looked pathetic. Although nothing but the vase had been broken in the search, it was going to take an entire day just to set things in order. Shea wondered again who might have done this and why. Even more to the point, how did the intruder enter the house? Berta was always extremely careful. She would never have left a door unlocked. Shea knew that she had her key, and her grandmother's key had still been in her purse when it was returned to her. On an impulse, she went downstairs and looked at the extra keys which were always kept in the kitchen drawer next to the sink. They were missing.

I need to call David, she thought. And I need to get these locks changed.

"George, let's stop at Jorge's Diner on Main Street and get some dinner," she suggested. "I'm starved, and it's on me."

"No, you don't," he said. "You bought grub last time. I'll pay for it."

Reluctantly Shea agreed, even though she was loath to let George, who lived on social security and a small pension, foot the bill. But George had his pride.

Jorge's Diner was next to Johansson's Market where Shea and her grandmother had shopped for years. Although the Super Store on the Highway had cheaper prices, the Market had fresher fruits and vegetables, many of which came from local farmers.

"Do you ever see Leland Johansson working there anymore?" asked Shea.

"Nah. The man's become too uppity," said George as they headed for a booth. "It reminds him of his earlier, poorer days. He never went to the restaurant much neither. Hangs out over at that feed and grain of his all the time. Maybe it makes him feel like a real powerful jefe. Now let's see what this namesake of mine has to eat."

Jorge's Diner was famous for its chile rellenos which were ordered by both Shea and George. After a satisfying meal, George dropped Shea off at Mary's apartment.

"This place looks awful fancy," he said.

"It's pretty nice, but I'll be glad when I can move back home."

"Don't David De Vargas live here?"

"Yes, he does."

When George pulled away from the parking lot, he was still grumbling.

"Shea, what would you be wanting to have for dinner?" Mary asked as she opened the door for her houseguest.

"Mary, I'm so sorry. I stopped with George for dinner."

"Then I'll just warm up some soup, and we'll sit down and have a bit of a chat."

When her mug was ready, Mary walked over to the sofa and sat at the opposite end from Shea, who was curled up and looking at a large book.

"What is it that you're so engrossed in, if you don't mind me asking?"

"It's a photograph album that belonged to my grandmother. I can't believe she kept so many momentoes of my sister and me. I've been looking at the photographs for days, reminding myself of better times. This is my sister and me dressed up to go to the rodeo. Look, here are our Vacation Bible School Certificates from St. Francis. We attended those every summer when we visited her. She even kept my graduation invitations from the University of Dallas and the University of Arizona."

Shea stopped as she noticed something clipped to the graduation invitation, which was the final page in the album. "Now what's this?"

Mary got up to look at the small scrap of paper. "It looks like a lottery ticket, me darling. Do you think it had some sentimental value?"

Slowly Shea drew the ticket from the page. She knew now why Joe had been killed. She also knew why the intruder had trashed Joe's house. He or she was looking for this ticket. Turning over the ticket, she saw that it was unsigned. She reached for the telephone just as it rang.

"Shea, this is David." He sounded very rushed. "I've been watching the evening news, and I think I've figured it out. I know why Dorothy was killed, and I know what they were looking for in her house."

"So do I, David. Can you come over?"

Aaron Kominski sat at his desk, which was remarkably neat and clean for a police officer, across from David De Vargas and Shea Chan. He looked completely unconvinced.

"So you think this woman was killed for a lotto ticket?"

"It's possible," said David, controlling his temper. "If a lottery ticket is unsigned, and someone finds it, then that person can claim it. Right now, the ticket is the property of Shea, because she was left everything that was in the house by Dorothy and all her financial assets."

Shea sat silently, waiting for Kominski's response. It certainly sounded plausible to her. She and David had discussed this in Mary's apartment for half an hour, and had continued arguing about it on the way to the police station. They both agreed that the lottery ticket was a possible motive for both the murder and the house break-in. What they couldn't agree on were the possible suspects. Shea didn't want to think that anyone who knew her grandmother would be capable of such a deed.

"Shea," said David with a practicality which she found infuriating, "money is a powerful motive. People have killed for much less."

"Ordinary, nice people like our neighbors and co-workers?"

"Yes, even neighbors and co-workers have murdered for a great deal of money."

And it was a great deal of money, Shea had learned. While watching the evening news when the lotto numbers were broadcast, David had written down the winning numbers and compared them to Dorothy's ticket. The numbers matched. There was no doubt that Shea held the winning ticket for millions of dollars. Under different circumstances, she would have been elated. At the present moment all she could think about was that this ticket might have cost her grandmother her life.

"The interesting thing is the date on the ticket. Dorothy bought it the day before she died," David was saying to Kominski. "She didn't even take the time to sign it. So there wasn't time for the news to get around that she had the winning numbers."

"That means," said Kominski, "that Hector Lopez found out about it somehow and then killed her for this ticket. After all, Dorothy was at the restaurant that night. She didn't even have time to call her granddaughter to tell her. Maybe she mentioned it at work. Now that I have a motive, I can get a confession."

"Don't you think we should question everyone who spoke to her that final day?" asked David.

"Do what you want," said Kominski with ill grace. "I know you'll go to the Chief anyway, and he'll back you up. He always does." Kominski waved the ticket in Shea's direction. "You'll get this back after it's entered into evidence. And I don't want you discussing this with anyone."

Kominski remained at his desk to record the evidence himself while Shea and David returned to the main room. Helen, who functioned as both night clerk and dispatcher, looked over and smiled at them.

"Would you like some coffee?" she asked sweetly.

For once, Shea was too wired up to accept her favorite beverage.

"No, thanks, Helen," she said. "But I really want to thank you for the sweater and booties. I promise I'll be sending out thank-you notes very soon."

"I won't feel safe until you've taken that ticket to Austin for redemption," David said in an undertone after Helen returned to her typing. "Would you like to wait while I call the Chief?"

"No, I don't mind. But I would like to notify Jason Tyler. I could really use his advice right now."

"Just let me check it out with Beau. If he says it's okay, we'll call Mr. Tyler. Chief, this is David. I'm down at the station. Aaron and I have something that you should see. It could mean a whole lot to the O'Daniels investigation." He paused. "Okay."

He turned back to Shea. "He'll be here in fifteen minutes."

"David, the last persons who saw Dorothy were Marlene and Hector, right?"

He nodded. He was thinking along the same lines, trying to imagine the final people who had come into contact with Dorothy along with the times and places.

"But that doesn't mean that Marlene and Hector knew about the ticket. Or it could mean that Dorothy told one of them or both of them, and they mentioned it to someone else."

Again David nodded.

"So that means," said Shea with a sigh, "that the possibilities are still endless. It literally could have been anyone who knew about the ticket and who came to steal it while she was alone in the restaurant."

This time he shook his head.

"Why not?"

"According to Hector and Marlene and everyone else, Dorothy always locked the door behind the last person to leave. That morning I found her was the first time I ever found the back door unlocked. That would mean that the person who entered the restaurant had a key. It also explains why they were able to come in without her noticing anything and to get close enough to her to shoot her."

"Then that means that the person who killed Dorothy knew her."

"That's exactly what it means," said David.

"What if she opened the back door for someone?"

"It would have the same result. Dorothy would not open it for a stranger, only someone she knew."

"That reminds me," said Shea. "Today while I was at the house getting some clothes, I checked for the extra keys that were always kept in a kitchen drawer. They were missing."

"Were they there before the funeral reception?"

"I'm not really sure," said Shea, trying to remember. "I just didn't think to look."

Kominski chose that moment to return with Shea's ticket. "If I were you," he said with a twist of his mouth, "I'd sign that sucker right now."

"Evening, y'all," said Chief Cummings who had just entered the reception area.

Shea noticed that Kominski's demeanor changed subtly the moment Beau entered the station house. The investigator seemed slightly deferential and certainly more respectful than he was of anyone else.

"Helen, that coffee smells great. Would you mind bringing me a cup? Now why don't all of you join me in my office."

David and Shea followed Kominski into Beau's office. Three sides of the room and the ceiling were panelled with white-washed pine while the fourth side contained the door and a huge picture window. Beau always said that he liked to keep an eye on his officers and all the visitors they had.

Shea had never been inside the Chief's office before, and she looked around admiringly at the mounted fish, framed certificates, and engraved plaques. Not one, but several framed photographs of the Chief's wife and children, all adults with children of their own, cluttered his desk. The desk was also littered with papers, pens, and a couple of coffee mugs. On the hat tree which stood in a corner, the Chief carelessly tossed his patrolman's hat alongside a baseball cap, a battered cowboy hat, and a hunting cap.

"Now Aaron, why don't you tell me what's up? I believe that David has some sort of disagreement with you?"

Darting a fierce glance at David, Kominski proceeded to describe the new evidence and the importance it had in an indictment against Hector Lopez.

"It's obvious that Lopez overheard the old lady saying something about her big winnings," he said, ignoring the fact that Shea flinched at the words 'old lady.' "Then he saw his opportunity when everybody left. He went back, killed her, and took her purse. When the ticket wasn't in the purse, he became enraged and threw her things away. He never thought we'd go looking for them. Then he gets out on bail. The funeral reception is held at Dorothy's house, and Shea goes to the hospital on the same night. He sees another opportunity. The ticket must be somewhere in the house. So he goes over, thinking that noone is there and finds Berta. He knocks her out, ties her up, and vandalizes the house."

"Well, David, you have to admit, that is a real plausible scenario," said the Chief as he accepted his coffee from Helen. "Hector had motive and opportunity, both times. And there is some serious evidence against him, especially since the ticket has turned up."

"I know how it looks, and I could be wrong," said David. He really didn't want to irritate Kominski more than necessary. "But on the other hand, it could have been a number of other people. Just because they're friends of hers, doesn't mean that the other restaurant employees didn't have opportunity or motive. For both crimes."

"All right, fellows, here's the drill. Kominski, you continue to press Hector. He may yet spill something that could be helpful. And let's use the polygraph."

That meant calling in Gary Armstrong, thought David. Armstrong, who was on patrol tonight, handled all the technical aspects of investigations.

"David, you draw up a list of persons to question. This time bring them down to the station house, starting tonight. And tell each one if we don't get the answers we want, that they could face a polygraph test as well. Of course, they can refuse," mused the Chief, "but it wouldn't look good. Aaron, I want you in on these interviews."

Kominski left the room looking none too happy. He thought he had wrapped up this investigation.

"As for you young lady," said the Chief so sternly that Shea looked up in surprise, "you are going to be a very wealthy young woman. So this is what we're going to do. Right now, I don't want a whole bunch of people knowing about this. My officers need some time to do a little poking and digging, if you know what I mean, and they don't need any distractions. So I'm going to call the Lottery Office in Austin myself and tell them that you are coming. I'm going to tell them that they should process this ticket with complete confidentiality. There will be no publicity until I say so."

92

"Thank you, Chief." Shea was certainly relieved. Publicity was the last thing she needed at this point.

"Now who's going with you?"

David cleared his throat. "Um, Chief, I think if we hire Scott Hathaway to fly us to Austin in his private plane that we could be there and back before my next shift."

"Why am I not surprised?" said the Chief with feigned innocence.

"Beau, could I tell Jason Tyler about the money? I think I'm going to need his advice on how to handle all this."

"I'll call him myself. Now if you don't mind, I would like for David to take you home. He has some work to do."

While making up her bed, which was actually the sofa, the next morning at the ungodly hour of four o'clock, Shea also concocted a story about some family business in Dallas to tell both Mary and the hospital.

"I'll be taking one of those small charter planes, but I'll probably be back by dinnertime," she said.

"Tis a hard time you're having, for sure," said Mary with such sympathy that Shea felt guilty. She would make it up to Mary, she resolved. Perhaps Mary would agree to be the live-in health care provider that Mark needed. Shea could now afford to pay more than the hospital paid her as a nurse's assistant, and she could throw in room and board to boot.

David had already made the flight arrangements with Scott, who was an old friend of his and who had agreed to keep their destination a secret. When David picked up Shea, she was wearing a white knit short skirt and boxy tunic with flat white sandals.

"You look great," he couldn't help saying.

Shea smiled at the compliment, but didn't think much of it. David probably said it to a lot of girls. Probably younger, prettier girls, she thought, who hadn't just given birth. It took them forty minutes to drive to the small private airport where Scott Hathaway kept his airplane. Just before they boarded the two-engine Cherokee airplane, Shea heard her cell phone ringing. Since Mark had been born, she was glad that she hadn't relinquishedthis luxury, because it kept her in constant touch with the hospital. George, of course, never called her on it, because he could never remember the number, no matter how many times she told him. She wondered who it could be.

93

"Shea, Jason Tyler."

"I'm glad you called, Mr. Tyler."

"Yes, I just spoke with Chief Cummings." Jason was one of the few people who addressed the Chief so formally. "He told me about your good fortune. If you like, I can contact bank officers today who can advise you about your money. I would certainly recommend CD accounts until you have some time to consider everything."

"I'll do whatever you recommend. I was thinking of asking for one lump sum."

"That would probably be best. Then you could invest the money more efficiently. I'll contact my accountant, and we'll work out the details concerning taxes."

Shea punched the off button, mentally blessing Jason for his professional concern and tact. Anyone else would have asked a million questions. Jason just handled the immediate issues.

Although the flight was relatively short, just under two hours, it was still early when Shea and David arrived in Austin. They took a taxi to the car rental place where Kyle had arranged for a rental compact. By the time that they drove to the Lottery Office, an official was waiting for them. He took them to a private office. No one else seemed to notice their presence, so Shea was pretty sure that the confidentiality agreement was being respected.

In a short while, Shea had presented the necessary documents, including the ticket, a driver's license, and a birth certificate, signed some forms for electronic transferral of funds, and shook hands with the officer.

"Your Chief Cummings is pretty well known with law enforcement agencies here," said the middle-aged gentleman. "Whatever he says goes apparently."

"Apparently," Shea agreed.

As they walked back to their rental, David said, "I think we could take a little more time. Would you like to have some lunch? On me."

Shea smiled. She had insisted to Beau that she would pay for the charter plane and car rental.

"It seems like I should buy lunch," she said. "After all I did get a free police escort."

"You can buy lunch next time," he insisted. "There's a great place right next to Lake Austin. We can sit out on deck and have a drink to celebrate."

"Sounds great," Shea said, perfectly willing to be convinced.

While they ate lunch, fried calamari and grilled shrimp, they tried to avoid the subject of the murder investigation for awhile. David told her about some of his experiences as a high school track athlete, in the mlitary, and at the police academy.

"Of course I'm just telling you about the clean stuff, you understand," he said when he had Shea laughing hard enough that he was sure she had forgotten about the investigation. "Some of the things we guys pulled on each other I just couldn't repeat."

"Isn't your mother here, David?" Shea asked, suddenly remembering that he had mentioned her once before.

"Yes, she is, but I don't think we'll have time to stop by today. She's in a suburb outside of Austin. It's actually a really nice place. Their home adjoins a country club."

"So your stepfather does really well?"

"He's an investment counselor, and yes, he does really well. I see them occcassionally. He's a nice guy, but we're not close."

Shea had been combing her mind for a memory of David's father. It seemed to her that he had died in the line of duty. She wanted to ask about him, but she felt she might be treading on thin ice.

"Everytime I see my mother, I'm reminded of my father," David said unexpectedly. "I don't mind that she remarried. It's only natural. It's just that he's so different from my father."

"What was he like? Your father?"

"Like Beau Cummings in some respects. Very well liked, well respected. But quieter. He didn't drink much or hang out with the guys much. He liked to come home, fix things around the house, watch football or baseball games. I think he would have loved it if he could have had a houseful of boys. But they had three girls before they had me."

"Did they turn out to be tomboys?"

"They're the most feminine, piano-playing, ballet-dancing girls you could ever meet. My oldest sister studied art and then married a psychiatrist. They live in New York. My next sister was a music major. She's not married and plays the cello in the Seattle Symphony Orchestra. My third sister was a teacher. She married a teacher. They live in Denver."

"That's quite a talented family."

"Which explains why I'm probably the only cop in West Texas who can tell the difference between a Chopin and a Bach sonata. I also know that 'Romeo and Juliet' isn't just a Shakespearean play, it's also a ballet. And if you tell anyone any of this, I will deny it. Then I'll hunt you down like a dog."

"All of that is safe with me. We all have our secrets. If you ever decide to come out of the closet, maybe we could catch a concert at the college."

Shea spoke casually enough, but David looked at her warmly. "It's a deal."

"Did you manage to question anyone last night?" she asked to change the subject, which was making her uncomfortable.

"No, I was on patrol. And we had a problem over at Hudson's Tavern. People partying a little too much."

On the return trip, David, who had been awake all night, was exhausted. He took the back seat to rest while Shea sat in the front and talked to Scott.

"So," he said when he thought David was safely asleep, "are you two a couple?"

"Not at all," said Shea firmly.

"Maybe you would like to go out sometime?"

Shea looked for a way to politely refuse him. "I just had a baby. I'm not dating right now."

"Okay," he said agreeably. "I'll try later."

Not if I can help it, thought David who had been eavesdropping from the back seat. He decided to stay awake for the rest of the flight.

After David dropped her off at the hospital, Shea went straight to the Intensive Care Nursery to hold Mark. She hadn't seen him all day.

"Hi, Shea," said Vanessa MacKenzie. She had walked in just as Shea was handed the small bundle she called her son. "I have some good news. Mark is doing so well that we could let him go home in two days. Here is the name of a medical equipment company that can provide you with all the equipment you will need."

"That's great."

"Have you managed to find some in-home health care?"

"I'm working on it," Shea was able to tell her with a smile. "Things are looking much better."

When Dr. MacKenzie left, Shea sought out Mary and asked if she could take a break. In the hospital restaurant, Shea bought coffee for herself and tea for the older woman. She then told her the story which she and Jason had devised until they were able to reveal the news about the lottery winnings.

"It seems that my grandmother had some bonds which were

left in a safety deposit box. And according to the will, I am the ben-
eficiary. So I am going to have more than enough money to take
care of Mark."

"Well, tis happy I am for you. I suppose that means you won't be
needing a boarder after all?"

"Actually, I was hoping that you would come to live and work
full-time at the house. I really need someone who has experience
around babies to help me. And you sure know a lot about medical
equipment and procedures. I could match your hospital salary and
then some."

Mary looked at her with complete disbelief. "Are you daft, me
girl? You don't have to pay me, at all, at all. I would take care of
that baby for free. Room and board is enough."

"We can discuss the details later, Mary. As long as you agree
to come."

David managed to catch a few hours sleep before getting up to
take a shower. He wanted to make a couple of stops prior to his
shift. He dressed, brewed a single cup of coffee, and made a quick
phone call. When he left, he paused long enough on the second
landing to see if he could manage a glimpse of Shea in Mary's
apartment. It didn't look as if anyone was home. She was probably still at the hospital visiting her baby, he thought.

Because he wasn't officially on duty, David drove his small
Jeep to the Highway and then headed toward an area on the edge
of town known as "The Junction." Years ago when trains had con-
ducted more business than they did at present, the railroad had
built a neighborhood of company homes. Once a thriving community with its own church, school, and stores, the area now furnished
run-down homes at cut-rate rental prices to struggling families.

Most of the homes had weeds and broken-down cars in the
front yards. A few even had broken windows.

David parked in the driveway of the second home on the first
street. At least here the renters made some effort. The front yard
was neatly mowed, and the front porch had been recently painted.
David knocked on the door which was promptly answered.

"Oh, yes, you're the officer who called," said the middle-aged
woman who answered the door.

"Yes, ma'm," said David as he entered the house. "You said
that you could give me some information about the night of

Dorothy O'Daniels' funeral."

From his front room where he was cleaning his Remington deer rifle, a 700 bolt action calibre .270, Bob Crockett heard the crunching sound loud and clear. Good thing I paved that drive with fresh gravel last spring, he thought. Dang thing works just as good as a doorbell to let me know who's coming. He went out to the small front porch just as a Texas park ranger was exiting his jeep. It was late evening, and the only light in the isolated area came from the cabin's window and the stars.

"Howdy," said Bob who didn't recognize the ranger. Must be new, he thought.

"Hello. Are you Mr. Bob Crockett?"

All these fellows sound college educated these days, thought Beau. And they're younger than chicken eggs. "Yep, that would be me."

"Sir, we received a call a couple of days ago from the Mesa Police Department. They would like for you to return and answer a couple of questions."

"What kind of questions, son?" From long experience, Bob was always reluctant to spend much time around the law, not even Beau Cummings whom he really liked and with whom he had gone fishing a couple of times. The Chief was one fine bass fisherman.

"It seems that after the funeral reception, which you attended, a Ms. Berta Rivera was attacked, and the house where she was staying was vandalized."

"Well, damnation, why didn't you say so in the first place? Somebody hurt Berta? Jesus Christ! Of course I'll go back right now."

"Mr. Crockett, did you kill any deer?"

"Didn't have no luck this time around."

"Did you catch any fish?"

"Nope, didn't take my rod or my reel with me."

"Chief Cummings also asked us to talk to Marlene Jankovitch. He would like to ask her a couple of questions as well."

"Marlene? Now you've got me boy. Beats me where that woman is."

Shea was asleep on Mary's sofa when her cellular telephone

rang. Grabbing it from her purse before it could awaken the older woman, she pressed the 'on' button. At the same time she glanced at her wristwatch. It was 3:42 a.m.

"Hello?"

"Shea?"

"Yes, it's me. Who is this?" Shea could barely understand or hear the voice on the other end.

"It's my fault, it's all my fault."

"Who is this? What's your fault?"

"Dorothy."

By now Shea could tell that it was a woman, but it was hard to identify the voice, because the caller sounded both drunk and hysterical. The woman kept crying loud gulps between words.

"Marlene, is that you?"

She was talking into a dead line.

Jorge's Chile Rellenos

12 long green chiles	4 egg whites
12 ounces shredded cheddar cheese	4 egg yolks
1 large onion, diced	1/2 t salt
1/2 cup flour	Vegetable oil

1. Heat chiles under broiler, scorching slightly on both sides. Remove skin.
2. Slit open chiles, remove seeds. Stuff chiles with cheese and onion mixture.
3. Roll in flour.
4. Beat egg whites until stiff. Beat yolks separately. Fold yolks into egg whites and add salt.
5. Dip flour-coated chiles in egg batter.
6. Deep fry chiles in oil at 360-365 degrees until golden brown.

La Mesa Noticia, Tuesday, June 11

Letters to the Editor

Can't the Mesa Roadhouse get a decent cook? I don't care if the police do think that Mexican boy killed someone. He was a d----d good cook. The new one has almost killed two or three customers with her cooking, and no one's arrested her for attempted murder.

H. H. (Name Withheld)

I've been a teacher for thirty years, and I find it appalling that we don't encourage more of our young Hispanic students to finish high school and attend college. The drop-out rate for Hispanic students in this region is much higher than the state or national average. We should encourage these young people to stay in school and improve their economic status.

Sonia De Vargas

Why are the toads so bad around here? Can't the city or the county do something about them? People should get together and demand that the toad problem be handled.

Edna Grunderson

(Editor's Note: Doctors at Mesa Medical Clinic report that Ms. Mabel Harding had taken an *antacid* tablet with a *Coca-Cola* not *acid* and *coke* as was reported on Sunday. Ms.Harding's stomach pains were caused by a bleeding ulcer.)

CHAPTER SEVEN

"This house is a mess," said George.

"You said that already," replied Shea.

George had been grumbling all day as they straightened drawers, replaced cushions and hung up clothes that had been flung from closets. His irritability was exceeded only by Shea's complacent mood. She was feeling better than she had in weeks mostly because of her noontime visit, the second in her day, with Mark. The Intensive Care nurse on duty had given her the good news that if the baby's progress continued, she was sure that Dr. MacKenzie would allow him to go home the following day.

"There's no reason he can't use the home respiratory equipment," the nurse told Shea. "Have you received it yet?"

"As a matter of fact, the company is delivering the oxygen machine and all the other equipment this afternoon. So I should be ready for the baby after that."

Her second good bit of news was when she went to check on Berta Rivera and was told that she had been released. Her friend Graciela Menendez had taken her to her mother's house. Later that day Shea and George had dropped by the home with a fruit basket which Berta's elderly mother had promptly appropriated.

"Ay Dios mio," sighed Berta after her mother had left the bedroom. She was propped up in bed surrounded by several fluffy pillows and a television remote. On the nightstand, Shea noticed a pitcher of water, a glass, and a prescription bottle. Gracie had taken care of everything. "I just can't believe that someone in this town would do such a thing. Are you going to be all right, mi hijita? Aren't you afraid to stay in that house alone?"

"I'm going to be fine. And I've hired a nurse's aide to help with Mark. She'll be living with us and helping round-the-clock. As a matter of fact, she's moving in today."

Mary had told Shea that she would be giving notice at the hospital and staying only as long as it was necessary to replace her. With a newly-graduated crop of candy-stripers, that shouldn't take

101

long, she said.

"And who is this woman?" Berta demanded. "Can she cook? Can she clean house? Will she take good care of you?"

"She's a lady I met at the hospital, a very experienced nurse's aide and very good with babies. Don't worry," Shea assured the housekeeper, "when you return from your vacation in Guanajuato, I will still want you to come clean and cook for me."

"Weekly? Si?"

"Daily if that's what you want. You don't have to work for anyone else ever again."

She left Berta with George for a moment and went to search for Berta's mother. Before she had left the house, she had filled an envelope with a number of fifty dollar bills which she had withdrawn from the bank for that purpose. Although she knew that Berta would refuse any financial help, Shea knew that the octogenarian would be much more practical. After all, Berta was unable to work right now, because she had been helping Shea.

Later Shea called the hospital and told them to send the Rivera bill to her. If the billing clerk, who had earlier encountered a much more penny-pinching young woman, seemed surprised, she didn't show it. Shea credited this lack of curiosity to Jason Tyler who was carefully spreading rumors, which didn't take long to spread in Mesa, that those stocks and bonds inherited from her grandmother were worth much more than he had originally thought.

Shea had also spoken to David De Vargas who assured her that the investigation was proceeding well. It had taken her only a few minutes after her early morning telephone call to locate him. Helen had tracked him down at the river levee where he was telling some high school kids that they had better pack it up and go home.

"So you think it was Marlene?" he asked over the car telephone.

"I can't be sure. Whoever called me had been drinking heavily and was crying really loud. But who else could it be?"

"Probably was her. Unfortunately there's no way to track the call now. Did you hear anything in the background?"

Shea thought for a moment. "Just some traffic, some horns blowing, that sort of thing."

"She was probably in a city," said David. "Perhaps in a motel room. Have you taken care of those new locks yet?"

"It's on my long list of things-to-do for today," she told him.

In fact, the locksmith had just finished changing locks on both the front and back doors. Shea gave George, who always had an extra set of house keys, his pair of keys and put Mary's keys in her grandmother's bedroom which she had just freshened up for the nurse's aide. Fresh flowers in a green vase from Alana's Flower and Gift Shop sat on the antique marble-topped dresser and helped create a more cheerful atmosphere.

A third set of keys went into her desk in her bedroom, and a fourth pair went into her purse. She intended to give those to someone she trusted the most.

"Are you ready to take all those boxes to your truck?" Shea asked George.

"Might as well. Got to get rid of 'em sometime."

Grabbing a large ox of clothes each, they carefully felt their way downt he stairs to place them in the truck bed. It took three more trips until they had emptied the study, which now only contained Shea's desk, chair, computer equipment, and her own boxes of books and personal items.

The nursery fared a little better. Shea had simply called up the local department store, La Fonda, and asked if they could deliver some baby items. When the salesperson said they could have the things delivered in the morning, Shea ordered a top-of-the-line baby bed, mattress, linens, chest, changing table, and two baby monitors. For her room, however, where she wanted the baby to sleep at night, Shea decided to use one of the family heirlooms.

"It's a good thing I done brought that old cradle down from the attic, because if I hadn't, it wouldn't get done," said George.

"I'll reward you. After we visit Mark this evening, I'll buy you dinner at Hudson's Tavern."

"Well, at least they still got good food there. The Roadhouse is all but ruined since they lost both their cooks."

"Isn't Bob coming back?" asked Shea.

"I think he's back. I saw that big Hog of his," said George, referring to the Harley-Davidson that Crockett usually rode. "But it was parked in front of the police station. That don't look good for Bob."

No, it didn't, thought Shea. Did the police suspect the burly, good-natured cook of doing something? Was he capable of murder?

❖

"Aw, come on, boys. You know I wouldn't hurt Berta. That sweet, itty-bitty thing," said Bob, referring to a woman who was almost as wide as she was tall.

"Didn't you and she have an argument earlier in the day?

103

Before you left town?" asked Kominski who wondered if the tattooed, bearded man could even read. Bob was sweating voluminously through his tee-shirt,which could mean that he was either incredibly nervous or suffered from high-blood pressure. Maybe both, thought Kominski without sympathy.

"That wasn't no argument. She just told me to get out of the kitchen. I was just trying to help, but she didn't see it that way."

"So you were in the kitchen?"

"Yeah, I just said so."

"That's when you took the keys to the house?"

"I didn't steal no keys, I done told you that. Why would I steal the keys?"

"You know why. You tell me what you were looking for in that house."

"I didn't go back there," insisted Bob. "I left for my cabin that night."

"With Marlene Jankovitch?"

"Right."

"What time was it when you left? Was it after you knocked out Berta?"

"We left at about eleven o'clock. And I don't know nothin' about what happened to Berta."

"Where were you before you left?"

"Drinking at Hudson's Tavern. I asked Marlene if she wanted to go up to my cabin and go fishin', and she said sure, she'd give it a try."

"So where is she now? Did she get cold feet?"

Kominski stood up and towered over Bob who was seated at the brown folding table which they used for interrogations. The cook sat nervously kneading his hands together which caused his heavy, muscled forearms to flex and resulted in the anchor tattoos swaying back and forth.

"The Park Rangers don't have any record of you paying at the gate to the park," said Kominski when Bob didn't answer.

"I got a yearly pass. They just wave me through."

"So what time did you get there?"

"Bout one o'clock, more or less."

"So this was after you attacked Berta?"

"I keep telling you man, I didn't attack no one. Don't he understand English?" Bob asked David, who had been standing quietly in a corner during the questioning.

"Where is Marlene, Bob?" asked David. "She wasn't at the cabin."

"We had a fight along the way. She said she didn't want to go nowhere with me. So I let her out at one of those rest stops on the Interstate."

"You left her there alone?" asked David. "In the middle of the night?"

"You don't know how that woman gets when she's mad. She can take care of herself. She's been in worse spots. She said she would call someone for a ride?"

"Did she call someone?" asked Kominski.

"I made sure she was on the telephone before I took off. Yeah, she was calling someone."

"Well, she's missing now, fellow. And you're the last one to see her. How come all the women you're around are getting hurt lately?" asked Kominski with cold anger. "First, there's Dorothy O'Daniels. You work at the restaurant with her. You could have gone back late at night and murdered her. Then there's Berta. You knew she would be all alone; then she was knocked out and tied up. You're a pretty big guy, Bob. It would be an easy job for you. Finally there's Marlene. You take off with her, and she suddenly disappeares. What did you do to her?"

Listening quietly David had to admire the tactics that Kominski was using. The investigator already knew that Marlene was still alive, because David had informed him of the early morning telephone call to Shea. By pretending that he didn't know, Kominski was hoping to catch Bob in some inconsistencies. Unfortunately, it didn't work.

"I swear I didn't do nothin' to any of those women. I ain't never hurt a woman."

"We know that you have an arrest record, Crockett. For assault. You did time."

Bob sat still for a moment. It was as if he had been expecting this.

"I only done three months in county jail, down in Georgia. I got in a fight with a guy in a bar. He come at me with a broken bottle, and I swung at him. He went down hard and broke his back. Ended up in traction. It was self-defense, but the judge didn't see it that way."

"You know a lot about fighting, don't you? And about guns. How many do you have? Half a dozen, a dozen? Don't you own a Smith and Wesson?"

Kominski put a registration paper in front of the cook. David knew that it was a copy of a sales receipt for a Smith and Wesson that had been purchased four years ago.

"It was stolen three weeks ago. I had it in my motorcycle bag. It was stolen while I was at work."

"You had opportunity, Crockett, and you had motive." Kominski acted as if he hadn't heard a word that Bob had just said.

"What motive?"

David noticed that Bob couldn't look straight at the detective as he had done with his earlier answers. Instead Bob averted his eyes and lowered his head.

Kominski pulled up a chair, turned it around and sat down. He took his time while he rested his arms on the back of the chair and got comfortable. His casual demeanor seemed to shake Bob just a little.

"Come on, Crockett. You know what motive. All you folks in that restaurant knew about Dorothy's good fortune. Don't pretend any more. You just couldn't stand it, could you? The thought of all that money? What did an old woman like Dorothy O'Daniels need with such loot? Not like you. You have lots of needs, don't you?"

Bob's head went lower until it almost touched the table.

"So this is how it went. You shot Dorothy for what you thought she had in her purse. Then when you couldn't find what you wanted, you put the purse and the gun in Hector Lopez' trash can. You set him up. The day that Dorothy's funeral was held, you went to the reception and stole the key. Then you returned to the house. Unfortunately Berta was still there. But you took care of her real good. You knew that Hector would be suspected again, because he was out on bail. Then you took off with Marlene so you would have an alibi. She was probably so drunk by that time she didn't know what time you guys left."

"It's all lies," said Bob between clenched teeth. "I want to talk to a lawyer."

Kominski stood up.

"White trash," he said to David as he was leaving the room. "Too bad we can't find both of them guilty."

After visiting Mark at the hospital, Mary, Shea, and George left for Hudson's Tavern. Shea had been elated when Vanessa MacKenzie, who had stopped by while she was feeding Mark, had told her that if the baby was doing this well in the morning, she could take him home.

"I understand that we're losing one of our best nurse's aides," Vanessa teased. "If I had known you were going to steal her, I wouldn't have suggested you need help."

"Why don't you join us for dinner?" suggested Shea.

"I'd love to, but tonight is Girl's Auxiliary at my church. First Baptist," she added when she saw George's perplexed look. "I teach Bible classes to eleven-year-old girls."

"Nice lady," said George when they left the hospital. Mary and Shea exchanged grins. That was really high praise from George.

At Hudson's Tavern, they headed for a booth. At this hour, the restaurant-bar catered to a quieter, more family-oriented crowd. A high chair at one table and a booster chair at another indicated the presence of babies and toddlers. As the night deepened, the families would give way to the younger crowds. On alternate nights there would be rock bands for the college crowd, western groups for the country-western fans, and salsa music for those inclined to more stylistic dance trends.

One could tell the music choice for the evening simply by looking at what the waitpersons, mostly college students from Mesa State University or Sul Ross at Alpine, were wearing. On country-western nights, the waiters and waitresses wore jeans and cowboy shirts. On rock and salsa nights, they wore jeans and tee-shirts. The young blue-eyed, blonde girl who came to take their orders wore a plaid shirt, black denims, and a silver bolsa tie.

"Do y'all know what you want?" she asked.

Shea didn't think the accent was faked. It sounded too pure. This was a home-grown college girl. George and Mary ordered beer while Shea asked for wine.

"Let's celebrate," she suggested as soon as they were handed menus, "and have the t-bones. And the shrimp appetizers."

"You're sure Miss Moneybags," said George as he returned his menu to the waitress.

"I lucked out, George. Joe left something behind that will really help out. Jason Tyler is investing those bonds so that I can live comfortably on the interest for the rest of my life."

Shea felt a pang of guilt over the white lies she was dishing, but she knew it was for the best.

"I'll drink to that," said Mary and lifted her mug. They all clinked glasses.

The three of them munched on shrimp stuffed with jalapenos until the tortilla soup arrived. That was followed by a huge t-bone steak accompanied by a sumptuous baked potato and a generous portion of cole slaw. Shea hadn't felt so hungry in months, and the food seemed to magically disappear on her plate.

"So why don't you use some of those investment earnings to

buy a new car?" asked George who was helping himself to a slice of Texas toast, an oversized piece of white break toasted with butter and garlic. "That jalopy you drive is not going to last much longer."

"That's a good idea," said Shea. "I think I can swing some monthly payments. Maybe buy something a little bigger than my Honda, like a Jeep Cherokee or a van."

While she listened to Mary and George debate the particular values of each type of car, she thought about the advice given to her recently by her lawyer. Jason, after conferring with his accountant, had assured her that her income from the lottery winnings, even after paying the initial taxes, could be invested in CD accounts and low-risk mutual funds to bring in an annual income of over one million dollars. This was after paying yearly taxes on interest, as well as accountant and investment counselor fees.

That was certainly more than she would ever need. Shea hoped that the present situation of confidentiality could continue indefinitely. At present only Jason, Beau, David, and Aaron Kominski knew the actual truth. Everyone else in town, including George, Berta, and Mary, thought her good fortune was due to the inherited bonds.

It would just make my life easier if it weren't public knowledge, thought Shea. The money was important to her, because now she could care for her infant son with ease. Feeling flush with money, she had ordered not one but two oxygen machines, one for the upstairs and one for the downstairs. Although the machines could be rolled from room to room, it would be difficult to take them up and down stairs. In addition to oxygen, the baby required an oxymeter to register and record his heart and oxygen rates. Portable oxygen units, now stored in the garage, had been provided as well. With a little instruction, Shea felt adequately prepared to operate and even clean the machine. She also felt relieved to learn that Mary was familiar with all the machines.

"I was saying me girl that we should work out a sleeping schedule. Is it daydreaming you'd be doing?"

"Sorry, Mary, I was daydreaming." Shea emphasized the word 'was'. "How do you want to do this?"

"Well, I was thinking you could buy one of those fancy baby monitors, you know, the one with a telly? Or maybe two. And we could have one in my bedroom and maybe one in the kitchen."

"I'm way ahead of you on that one," said Shea. "I ordered two of the best from La Fonda already. I had seen them in some of the baby catalogues and couldn't resist."

Shea had accumulated at least half a dozen specialty catalogues and was finding it extremely hard not to order every single
baby gadget that was advertised.

"I have only one more day at the hospital. They've been grand
about finding a replacement. So don't you know that I'll be able to
take the night shift so to speak."

"That's not really fair," protested Shea.

"Now listen, me girl. I'm an old woman. I don't need much
sleep. You're a young mother, and you'll be needing to do a lot of
things during the day, such as going to a doctor and what not. So
I'll stay awake from ten at night until six in the morning. Then you
can get up all refreshed like. I'll sleep a few hours. Then I'll nap
again in the late afternoon. That's how I like to do it best."

George listened with great interest to this take-charge woman.
"You'd better do it her way, kiddo. Or you'll never hear the last of
it."

"What will you do all night?"

"I'm used to working night shifts," said Mary with pride.
"Remember I've been a taxi driver and a waitress as well as any
number of other jobs. I like to knit and read and watch a bit of telly.
You do have cable, don't you?"

"It's connected in the living room. I can have it installed in your
bedroom if you like. How about dessert?" Shea asked with sud-
den enthusiasm.

"Where are you putting it?" asked George.

"She needs to put on some weight, for sure," said Mary. "She'll
be ordering the flan or some such thing, don't you know?"

Not one to disregard such excellent advice, Shea did indeed
order the pecan pie while George and Mary settled for coffee.

"Isn't that Curtis Fernshaw?" asked Shea when she spied the
long-haired teenager who was clearing the table next to them.

"Yeah, that's Hester's boy," replied George, who knew every
single person in town and then some. "His dad left 'em six months
ago. Good riddance I say. He used to beat all of 'em, the mother,
the son, and his younger brother."

Shea glanced again at the skinny, acne-covered, sixteen-year-
old. She wondered if that was why he looked angry and hostile.
Of course it could simply be teenage hormones.

"Why is he working here? I thought he bussed over at the
Roadhouse?"

"I heard that Leland Johannson fired him. Said he was stealing money from the cash register. So Freddy Hudson hired. him.
No love lost between Freddy and Leland, I can tell you that."

Shea paid the bill, and they left in separate vehicles, Mary in her station wagon, Shea and George in the truck. As George backed out of the parking lot, Shea saw Ceci De Anda entering the restaurant with a group of boisterous young people.

Line dancing tonight, she thought idly.

❖

At eleven o'clock, David De Vargas walked into the station to begin his shift. As usual Helen was at her desk, having already begun a fresh pot of coffee which she would keep going until she left at seven o'clock the next day.

"Have you heard that Shea Chan has just hired a live-in nurse's aide to help with her baby?" asked Helen, who uncovered news faster than CNN. "She's bringing home the baby in the morning. I'm so happy that Jason Tyler invested those bonds for her. No one needed them more."

"So what is the town saying about Shea's good fortune?" David asked innocently.

"Funny," she said, giving him an arch look, "I don't ever remember you being interested in gossip before."

He really wanted to know if the town was buying the story concocted by Jason Tyler. The fabricated story helped not only Shea, but also the police investigation. Beau Cummings was hoping that they might be able to use the lottery ticket as bait for whoever had killed Dorothy. Because by now, even Aaron Kominski had his doubts that Hector Lopez had shot her. After questioning Bob Crockett, they had been forced to release him. They had no real evidence to prove that Bob had either shot Dorothy or attacked Berta. The gun receipt which Aaron had used in his questioning had been a fake. It wasn't the receipt for Bob's gun. But at least they had learned that his gun had been stolen. And it was obvious that Bob knew aobut the lottery ticket and thought it was still unclaimed.

"Well, Alberto over at the bakery says that he knew all along that Dorothy O'Daniels had something put away. He says the O'Daniels always have a little something up their sleeves. He says he never knew them to be broke. And Edna Grunderson says she's just tickled pink that Shea is taken care of. Especially since she can stay in town now." Helen sent David a meaningful, sideways glance. "Don't you think that's nice?"

Grabbing his hat, David said he had to leave to patrol.

As usual he began his first swing around the perimeter of the city. Afterwards he always worked his way inward to monitor the quieter neighborhoods. Passing Hudson's Tavern, he slowed a bit to ascertain the number of cars in the parking lot. From the Tavern, he could hear the sounds of a country-western band playing a George Strait song.

Pretty quiet for a Tuesday evening, he thought.

He continued on Highway 52 until he came to Johannson's Feed and Grain. Tonight he could see no inner lights in the warehouse.

I guess old Leland doesn't work like a dog every night, he thought.

He checked out the Super Store on the highway which stayed open all night. Everything looked normal. There were always a few late-night shoppers or college students who liked to go there to take a break while they were studying for an exam.

He turned into Country Club Lane and drove along the dark country road which held mostly farmers and ranchers who turned into bed every night at ten. Country Club, however, led to the river levee which he definitely kep an eye on, especially during these long summer nights. Both high school and college-aged kids liked to hang out there. He liked to make sure that there wasn't too much drinking, and that there were not drugs. More than once he'd taken home a young girl who had decided that she no longer wanted to party.

Tonight, thank goodness for small favors, the levee was deserted.

David continued through the small town, observing the late night crowds which were leaving the movie theatre, the bowling alley, and the bingo parlor. This evening people were orderly and in a friendly mood. As he drove through residential neighborhoods, he always noticed which families preferred to stay up late and which families retired early. On Mulberry Drive, he slowed down to almost a complete stop. On the second floor, one bedroom light still shone. He wondered if that room belonged to Shea.

Was she staying awake thinking about her good fortune? Was she missing her grandmother? Of was she thinking about the baby she would bring home tomorrow. David hoped that it was the latter event which occupied her thoughts. Obsessing on the death of her grandmother was fruitless at this point. Better leave that to the professionals. As he finished the rest of his rounds, David reviewed what he knew and what he suspected. It seemed to him that the connection had to be between who was in the restaurant on the day that Dorothy died and who attended the funeral reception. He had already learned that Bob, Marlene, Ceci, Rosie, and Hector had all worked that day. Each of them had talked to Dorothy at some point. All of them but Hector had attended the funeral reception. Only Leland Johannson had not been at the restaurant on Saturday night although he had shown up at the funeral reception. Besides Leland had left early on Saturday to fly to Midland in his Cherokee airplane. David had checked, and his plane definitely left the hanger last Sunday before 8:00 p.m. Leland didn't return until the next morning at shortly after nine p.m.

Could he have heard something between the time of Dorothy's death and the reception to make him want to search the house? David doubted it. He knew that the employees were not friendly with Leland who seldom ever went to the restaurant. They would have no reason to share such information with him.

Which left the earlier suspects, thought David, who felt he was simply going in circles. He knew instinctively that Rosie and Ceci were hiding something. He also knew that Marlene Jankovitch felt guilty about something. And Bob Cummings ws downright scared. In fact, all of them were spooked.

Because he liked to check out all the late night businesses, he headed down the highway toward the Mesa Roadhouse. There were less than the usual number of semi-trailers, trucks, and cars in front of the restaurant.

Hester must be cooking tonight, he thought.

David was right on the money about one thing. Shea was sitting up, too excited to sleep. Mary had gone to bed hours ago, elated that tomorrow was her last day to work at the hospital and that Shea would have her son with her. George had also gone to his apartment after insisting that he would take Shea to pick up Mark.

"I can drive now, George. It's been almost a week," she had protested. After a bit, she gave up the fight. It was obvious that George was almost as excited as she was. He wanted to be there when the baby was released.

At the moment that David was driving past her home, Shea was sitting in her bed, reading. It was her favorite pastime along with music. If she became addicted to anything as a result of her new-found wealth, she thought, it would surely be books and CDs. Before she and George had arrived back at the house, they had stopped at the Super Store on Highway 52 where she had treated herself to several CDs and paperbacks. At that moment she really felt that for the rest of her life she could simply become a hermit in this house, enjoying her books, her music, and her new baby.

"You're going to have to build a room just to hold all them books," George said when she had finished with her shopping.

"Actually that's not a bad idea," said Shea. She had considered remodeling the house, but she felt she needed to consult an architect first. She really wanted to preserve the historical integrity of the place. Nevertheless, they really needed an additional bathroom, a master bedroom with a sitting area, and a larger study downstairs. Then she could use the present study for a guest room.

Finding that she couldn't really concentrate on the mystery novel, she set it aside and went downstairs where the television had cable. Flipping through channels, she searched for something that would occupy her mind and hopefully make her sleepy. She listened to the weather report, sports statistics, and then found a program which was based on real "victimless" or "white collar" crimes. Each of the episodes highlighted a very intelligent and calculating person who initiated a very unique and illegal criminal activity.

Well, this is interesting, thought Shea and settled down to watch.

Hudson's Flan

4 eggs	½ cup sugar
1 can sweet condensed milk	1 can evaporated milk
1 Tb vanilla	

1. Beat the eggs with the condensed milk. Add the evaporated milk. Beat well.
2. Heat the sugar and vanilla in a saucepan.
3. Pour syrup mixture into mold. Pour egg and milk mixture on top.
4. Place molds in shallow pan of water.
5. Bake at 375 degrees for one hour.

La Mesa Noticia, Thursday, June 13

Editorial

The population of Mesa is growing and thriving. The fine year-round weather and friendly atmosphere has attracted interest from a number of potential businesses who are considering relocating here from the east. One of the major problems, however, in obtaining a commitment from these businesses continues to be the lack of educational facilities. At present we have one high school, a junior high school, and two elementary schools. The number of children enrolled has outgrown all of these schools. It is time to consider passing a bond which will provide funds to build at least one more school at each level.

We urge voters to get on the bull and encourage our City Council to pass this bond. The bull is in your court. Don't drop the bull!

(Editor's Note: Wednesday's notice concerning the Globe Theatre should have read "Admission is free for all who *served* in World War II".)

CHAPTER EIGHT

"Okay, kiddo, now you've got to get a new car. That old one of yours died.

I tried it this mornin' and got nothin' but some screeches."

Shea, who had been concentrating on a delicious ham and cheese omelette prepared by Mary, looked up to see George stomping through the back door.

"Do you think we could get it to the car dealer for a trade-in?" she asked.

"Yeah, if a tow truck hauls it," he answered.

"That bad?"

"That bad, kiddo."

"Okay, I'll call Fitzgerald's New and Used Cars," she said.

She spent the next hour arranging for a tow for her dead Honda and calling the car dealer. When she called Fitzgerald's New and Used Cars, she asked to speak to Ralph Fitzgerald, the owner.

"Mr. Fitzgerald died last year," said the receptionist.

She knew she shouldn't be surprised. Ralph Fitzgerald was a contemporary of her grandparents. "Who's running the business?"

"Gregory Fitzgerald, his son. I'll put your through."

Shea had never met Gregory Fitzgerald, who was in his early thirties and portly with a ruddy complexion that suggested high blood pressure. He wore an ill-fitting checkered sports jacket and an outdated slender tie. Like everyone else in town, he knew her grandmother. He had also heard the still-circulating rumors about her bonds. The story was that was making the rounds was that she was comfortable but by no means wealthy. Accordingly he assumed a diffident manner that was suited to what he considered to be her financial means. His tone definitely suggested that he considered her to be a middle-of-the-range buyer.

"So you will be needing a new car. Something suitable for transporting a child?"

"That's correct."

"We can order anything you want if we don't have it on the lot.

How about a sports utility vehicle or a super-size van?"

"Actually what I had in mind was a little smaller, something like a Jeep Cherokee."

In fact Shea knew exactly what she wanted. For the past two years she and Mark had decided that their first purchase when he began his career would be a new car, one planned for a growing family. They had determined the type of car, the color, and the interior. Now she would have everything for which she had planned. Just not with Mark.

"Can you get it in a dark blue, not navy, not royal, more of a cobalt blue?"

"That should be no problem," answered Gregory.

She could hear him scribbling on a paper.

"What about other options?" He began to recite a long list of accessories.

Shea ordered most of the necessary options as well as a few luxuries such as a CD player and a car telephone. She drew the line, however, at racing stripes and designer hubcaps. She wasn't going to enter the car in a beauty contest. As she wrote out a down payment check, he folded his hands on his desk and looked at her thoughtfully.

"It will take about a week to have this delivered. We'll be ordering the car from our dealership in Midland. Now will you be needing a rental in the meantime? It's included as part of our service."

Why not, thought Shea. She needed to go to the beauty salon for a haircut and, there would be other errands to run during the week. She couldn't constantly be pestering George for lifts.

"I could use one. Could you have it delivered to my house?"

"Sure. We've just received something that's brand-new and really cute. I'll have someone take it over to you right now." Shea started to rise from her chair when Fitzgerald cleared his throat. "I just wanted to say how sorry I was about what happened to your grandmother. I was at the funeral and the reception, but it didn't seem the appropriate time to approach you."

Shea looked at him with bewilderment. Why should he need to approach her? What else was going on?

"I don't know if your grandmother ever mentioned it, but we're actually distant cousins. Your great great grandmother, Katharine Fitzgerald, was the sister of my great great grandmother, Martha Fitzgerald."

Visibly relaxing, Shea gave him a warm smile. "That's really great news. No, I don't think she ever mentioned it. Or if she did, I was too young to take notice. Although I do remember that she

116

was quite fond of your father."

"Yes, they kept in touch, always calling each other at least once a week. When you have some time, I believe there are old photograph albums in the basement with pictures of both women when they were young."

"I appreciate knowing that. Thank you for telling me."

"And if there's anything I can do for you, please don't hesitate to call," he said, standing and holding out his hand. "My wife and I will do anything we can to help."

Shea had noticed the framed photograph of his family, a nice-looking thirtyish woman and two small boys, both under the age of six. Thanking him again, she went out to the parking lot where George was waiting for her.

Within an hour, a teenage boy drove up to the curb of the house and hopped out of a hunter green Mustang convertible.

"These are cool," he said as he handed Shea the keys. "I'd like one of them. They drive real smooth, and they aren't nearly as expensive as other sport cars. This one's just a little nicer, because it's got that leather interior and a CD player and air conditioning. I think I'm going to save up for me. Only I'd like mind in red."

"Thanks for delivering it," said Shea, offering him a nice tip.

It was cool, she thought as she inspected the butterscotch leather interior and dashboard. She had never imagined driving a sports car before so this would be a new experience.

Deciding that she should dress a little more stylishly to do justice to the rental, Shea went to her bedroom to replace the tee-shirt and shorts she was wearing with a navy blue print sundress. It was a t-strap, flared dress that reached just above her knees. In one of her drawers she found a white cotton scarf to tie around her chin. Putting on her sunglasses, she surveyed herself in the full-length mirror on the closet door.

Sort of like Natalie Wood in 'Splendor in the Grass,' she thought. Or maybe not, she decided in a more realistic vein.

In the kitchen, Mary was simultaneously baking and keeping an eye on the baby monitor when Shea told her that she was leaving.

It's amazing, thought Shea, that Mary could sleep from nine to midnight last night, be up from midnight to six, sleep until nine, and be set for the rest of the day.

"I told you that I can sleep in spurts and be just as bright-eyed and bushy-tailed as anyone else who sleeps for eight hours," she had insisted. "I'll take me another nap this afternoon and be good as gold."

"Mark's been fed and changed," said Shea unnecessarily. Mary always seemed to know even if the monitor wasn't being used.

"I know me darling, and he'll be just fine. Go have yourself a little treat."

After driving the short distance to town with the top down, Shea enjoyed it so much that she was disappointed it didn't take longer. She had made an appointment that morning at Opal's Hair Salon rather than with the franchise studio at the Alpine Mall. She just didn't feel like dealing with crowds today.

"My, my, you look cute as a button, honey," said Opal when Shea entered the shop.

In her mid-thirties, Opal Garfield had dyed blonde hair, dark roots, and always wore shocking pink or deep red lipstick and nail polish. Today she was wearing jeweled cowboy boots, tight jeans, and a clinging pink cotton tee-shirt that revealed an abundance of cleavage. Opal had been divorced twice and claimed she was still looking for 'Mr. Right'.

"He's out there," she would tell her friend. "He's just taking his time to find me."

"I like this hairstyle, Shea," the beautician told her while she was shampooing the young girl's head. "We'll keep it like this, but I'll just trim off those dead ends. How about a nice manicure? Are you still biting your nails, girl? I've been trying to get you to quit tht ever since you came to my shop for the first time. You were only twelve that summer."

Opal kept up a running monologue while she washed and cut Shea's hair. Fortunately Shea didn't need to sit under a hair dryer, because her style only required a blow dryer. She half-listened to Opal discussing her problems with recent dates, a rather half-serious, half-funny monologue on the trials and tribulations of the single woman.

When she took a breath, Shea took advantage of the break to ask, "Opal, did you ever go to the bingo parlor with Marlene and my grandmother?"

"No, honey. That's for old folks. I like a little more excitement, like the rodeo and drag-racing. Someplace with a lot of hunky guys," she said with a knowing smile. "We gals have to make the best of the time we have. None of us are getting any younger. Of course, I won't go out with just anyone. I have my standards. No married guys or wife-beaters for me."

Shea had always liked Opal. She might be flashy and gregarious, but she was the real thing. She worked hard, never felt sorry for herself, and treated everyone the same, as if they were family. Her only problem was that she usually picked the wrong guys.

"So who have you been dating?" Shea asked. She needed to concentrate on someone else's problems for awhile. As Opal complied with tales of her most recent conquests, Shea listened with growing interest.

❖

"Come on David, say you'll do it," said Gary Armstrong into the telephone.

"I can't believe you woke me up to ask me this." David glanced at his alarm clock. It was a few minutes before two p.m. He had finally managed to get almost seven hours of sleep. "Gary, I'm really glad that you finally got the nerve to ask Vanessa out to dinner. And by the way, how did you manage that?"

"Remember that phony personal ad that Hank Hatfield put in the newspaper about me?"

David tried not to laugh. Hank, the department prankster, had been the mystery man behind a "singles" ad that claimed a single, jazz-loving, African-American male wanted to meet a single African-American female with the same interest. Gary had been alternately embarrassed and amused by the unwanted publicity and good-naturedly accepted a lot of ribbing. In the end it had paid off well for him.

"Some of the nurses at the hospital noticed the ad and kept kidding Vanessa about it. Apparently she really does love jazz. So one of them introduced me to her. I asked her to have coffee in the hospital cafeteria. While we were having coffee, I asked her to dinner."

"That's great, Gary. But how does that concern me?"

"Well, I'm still a little nervous with her. I mean, she's so well-educated and elegant. I think I'm out of my league here. If we could double-date, it would make things a lot easier."

"Gary, I don't have time to go on a double-date with you. I'm caught up in this investigation, and besides, I'm not going with anyone right now."

"You could ask Shea Chan. You and she are good friends. And it would be good for her to get out and go somewhere."

"Look man, she just lost her husband a few months ago and her grandmother a week ago. She's not in any mood to date."

"It wouldn't have to be a date. She would just be coming along to make it easier on Vanessa and me. Just like you will be doing.

Besides I know that Vanessa likes her a lot. We could go over to that Italian restaurant in Alpine."

"Why are you so nervous?"

"Why? Are you kidding? This is the most beautiful woman that I've ever met. Not only that but she's a doctor for God's sake! I'm just a policeman who probably makes one-fourth what she does."

You should know what my would-be date makes in a year, thought David.

"Okay, I'll ask Shea if she wants to go. But I'm not promising anything. Tomorrow night, you say? How did you swing it that both of us got the night off?"

"I'm blackmailing Jaime."

Jaime Chavez, the Assistant Chief, always made up the week-ly work roster.

"I'll call her and ask," David said. "But don't count on it."

Deciding that further sleep was useless, David got up from the couch which also functioned as his day bed and went to the refrig-erator. It was almost devoid of anything that resembled food although a couple of items looked like they were reproducing. Scrambling into jeans and a tee-shirt, he got into his jeep and headed for downtown. After a few minutes, he found a parking spot next to the plaza. As he started to enter Johannson's Grocery, he saw Shea coming out of Alberto's Bakery. She put a box in the trunk of her car, and then she began to walk in his direction.

Damn, she looks good, he thought. In a week's time she had lost most of the baby fat that mothers put on in their later months. Having been made an uncle four times over, he was familiar with the process. Her hair looked shiny and swingy, and as for that dress, wow. He was ready to ask her out now regardless of what he had told Gary.

"How are you doing?" he asked and nodded in the direction of the Mustang. "Nice car."

"It's a loaner. I had to order a new car, because mine finally gave up the ghost today. I bought a Jeep Cherokee. I think it will be the best choice for taking Mark to and from the doctor."

"It is a good choice," he said as he held the door for her to enter the market. They both took carts which they directed toward the produce section. "Very reliable. Not too big or overbearing for you. And it'll give you plenty of room for all that baby stuff you new moms carry around."

Why was he dithering? They both chose cantaloupes and oranges, carefully rummaging for the best choices.

"I wouldn't take that one," Shea told him as she rapped on the

120

cantaloupe shell. "It doesn't sound ripe."

"Okay," David said agreeably and put it back. Personally he thought it would go well with his other refrigerator inedibles.

"I need to ask you another favor," he began.

"Another one?" she said in a mocking tone. "Yesterday wasn't enough? Do you want me to adopt an orphanage? Feed Afghanistan?"

"This one won't cost you a cent," he said nobly ignoring her sarcasm. "It's really a favor for a friend. You see I've got this cowardly co-worker who has a crush the size of China on our mutual friend, Vanessa MacKenzie. He figures that since you two get along so well it would make things easier on him."

"Make what easier on him?"

"Well, he has finally gotten her to agree to go out with him. God knows why, but I suppose even doctors have temporary lapses of sanity. For dinner tomorrow night. He's taking her to Giuseppe's in Alpine. But he's paranoid about being alone with a woman who can use three-syllable words in a conversation. He figures if there are more people around, his lack of syntax and adjectives won't be so obvious. It will make the evening go more smoothly."

"And just how do I figure into this dysfunctional social outing?" Shea waved her hand in a circle as if to say, get on with it.

"He asked if I would double-date with him. And at present, there aren't a lot of names on my dance card. I just don't know who else to ask. All the women I know are either married or think I'm too annoying. So Gary and I thought you might agree to go. Heck, it's a free meal."

"Of course, I should have known," said Shea shaking her head. "Whenever anyone thinks of someone who'll do anything for a free meal, they think of me."

"That would be my guess."

"I don't know how I could refuse such a gracious and," she paused for effect, totally inexplicable offer. How long will this "date" take?"

Shea made quotation marks in the air with her fingers when she said the word "date."

He told her the time it would take to drive to Alpine.

"And dinner would be about an hour and a half?"

"Yeah, about that much."

"No dancing or movies afterward, right?"

Geez, she's a tough negotiator, thought David as he nodded silently. Somehow it takes all the romance out of the evening.

"No dancing, no movies," he told her. "Absolutely nothing beyond the required eating of the meal."

"Okay, then. It's just that, I still get kind of tired, and I really hate to be away from Mark for very long."

"I promise this won't become a habit.

"Is Giuseppe's a dressy place?"

"It's pretty nice," said David who had no idea what constituted 'dressy.' "Giuseppe's requires reservations if that helps."

"What time will you pick me up?"

"Seven o'clock. See you then."

While they were negotiating the finer points of the impending date, they had chosen groceries, moved through the cashier's line and paid for their respective goods. Outside Johannson's Market, David walked toward his jeep. Turning back for one last look at Shea, he saw her still carrying her brown paper bag filled with fruit and vegetables by the handle. Instead of walking toward her car, however, she turned into Edna's Boutique.

Good sign, he thought. I think.

In the boutique, Shea tried on several dresses, most of which she rejected as either too formal, too casual, too sexy, or too frumpy. Finally she found what she thought was the perfect dress for a dinner invitation with a friend. Slipping on a white jersey silk halter dress with a mid-calf hemline, she stepped outside the dressing room to get Edna's opinion. She draped the matching silk shawl around her shoulders. The dress was not tight, which was a good thing since she still had a tummy, and the soft, clingy material flowed nicely when she walked.

"That is just perfect, dear," said the shrewd businesswoman with approval. It was one of her pricier outfits. "You say this is for dinner at Giuseppe's? They have a nice, upscale clientele there, and this will fit right in. Do you have some jewelry to wear with it?"

Shea nodded. She intended to wear the simple pearl studs that Mark had given her for Christmas two years ago.

It's ironic, she thought to herself as Edna brought accessories for her to view, now that I can afford to buy anything I wish, including diamonds or other jewels, all I want are remembrances of other people.

"I won't need any jewelry, but I will take some shoes and an evening bag. Just nothing with sequins, please."

Shea left shortly afterwards for home, having spent a good

three hours of the afternoon downtown. It wasn't until she was turning into her driveway that she remembered something. She had meant to pass along to David a piece of information that Opal had given her.

Well, it's probably not anything important, she thought. It can wait until tomorrow night.

❖

When he arrived at work that evening, David saw Gary waiting for him with anticipation.

"How ya doin' pardner?" said David in an exaggerated imitation of a western drawl. He walked over to the coffeemaker.

"Would you mind cutting out the bull?"

"Okay. She said she would go. But we have a very tight time-line. She's got to be home by eleven or she breaks curfew and will be grounded."

"What?"

"Give her a break, Gary. She just had a baby. She's doing this as a favor to you."

"All right. All right. But I was hoping to get Vanessa to go to that new club in Alpine after dinner. I wanted to have a few drinks, do a little dancing."

"I'm afraid that's out for the new mom."

"Maybe we could take separate cars."

"Fine by me," agreed David.

"Oh, by the way. Judge Ayes signed the warrant this morning, and I got those phone records you requested."

David grabbed the sheets that Gary was holding and sat down at his desk to peruse them. Nothing looked very unusual. He scanned the sheets several times. One number, which was unfamiliar to him, was listed a half dozen times. When he dialed it, the phone rang several times with no answer.

"Is there a way to reach the telephone company at night?" he asked Gary.

"Nope. You'll have to wait until tomorrow morning. What do you need?"

"I need to know whose number this is?"

"Maybe I can find it on the computer. Give me a few minutes."

David waited impatiently, busying himself with some routine forms while Gary typed furiously away at the computer. In a few minutes, however, he was rewarded.

"Bingo, it's a pay phone in front of a liquor store on University

123

Avenue. Here's the address."

"Thanks, pal. I'll see you later," said David.

Ten minutes later he arrived at the liquor store. Because this was a college town, the place was constantly occupied and usually open as long as the law allowed. Young twenty-somethings and others who looked even younger roamed the aisles choosing packs of beer and wine coolers. Ignoring the suspicious looks which were cast in his direction, David walked to the pay phone in front of the liquor store. He noticed that the number on the telephone was the same one he had noticed six times over on the phone records.

Returning to the store, he approached a cashier wearing a Mesa State University tee-shirt.

"I'm Officer De Vargas," he said.

"Hey man, we don't sell to minors."

"That's not why I'm here," said David although now he suspected that the man did indeed sell to minors. "I'm looking for someone who has been using this pay phone a lot. It's usually late at night or early in the morning, just before you're closing. Can you think of anyone who would be a regular here?"

"We get a lot of people. Some of them are pretty weird, too. We can't keep track of that sort of thing."

David mentioned a couple of dates. The cashier frowned as he tried to remember.

"You know on those nights, I wasn't working," he said. "Cindy had those shifts."

"Can you give me an address where I can find Cindy?"

"She's out of town. But she'll be back on Monday. Try coming back then."

Not quite a dead end, thought David as he left in the police cruiser. But damn close to it.

On Friday Shea lazed around the house, so comfortable in tee-shirt and shorts that she was sorry she had ever agreed to go out on a dinner date that evening. After all it would mean making an effort to get ready.

Maybe I should call a dating service for a substitute, she thought idly as she sat on the front porch swing and watched George turning over soil to plant petunias. George was one of the best gardeners in the county, bringing Garden Club ladies to the verge of madness with his ability to grow the largest squash and the most exquisite roses in two states with very little effort.

After a while, Shea went back upstairs to bathe Mark and rock him to sleep. It was a sweet pleasure which she savored. When he was sleeping peacefully, she finished one novel and started another. On her discman, she listened to Albinoni and Bach. As she read and idly listened to the familiar music, she suddenly experienced the same anxiety she had felt in the hospital when listening to the same composers.

Something was nagging her at the back of her brain. Something elusive and intriguing. Eventually she gave up trying to recoup the memory.

I'll think of it sometime, she told herself.

Finally the hour approached when she had to get ready for the evening. She had decided to follow a procedure she read about in a magazine, so she took a luxuriating bath in the six-foot long Victorian bathtub, complete with bath salts and aromatherapy candles.

This is what women are supposed to do for dates now? she asked herself. It was easier back when Mark had been courting her. Actually it hadn't even seemed like dating when she was with him. It had been so easy, so natural, like breathing.

Fortunately she didn't have to do much to her hair, which was low maintenance, and her makeup didn't require a lot of time either. The most time-consuming task occurred when she had to decide about her wedding ring. Somehow it didn't seem appropriate to wear it, and yet she was loathe to relinquish the symbol. In the end, she decided to wear the ring on the chain which held her cross and would not be visible under the halter neckline.

Downstairs she paraded around for Mary and George.

"Don't you look grand!" exclaimed Mary.

"You look okay," said George. "Why do you have to go? Ain't we feedin' you enough here?"

"I'm trying to help out a friend of David's. He wants to impress a girl, actually Mark's doctor. You know that David has been working really hard and a lot of extra hours on this investigation lately. So it's the least I can do. Besides I'll be home early."

"You should stay as long as you want and kick up your heels a bit," said Mary.

"You should come home as soon as you've had your dinner," said George.

"I'm too tired to kick up my heels and besides they're too tired," Shea said to Mary while ignoring George's comment.

Shea went to the front door when she heard the doorbell ringing. David was standing there in a dark blue suit and burgundy striped tie. He walked into the foyer with a huge smile.

"Evening Mary. Evening George."

"Hmph," said George, stomping out the back door.

"You are looking fine this evening, Officer," said Mary. "Do you have your cell phone, me darling?"

"Got it, Mary. We'll see you later."

David opened the door to his khaki green jeep thinking that it looked rather shabby to be transporting someone who looked this good.

"I really appreciate it that you're helping out tonight," he said.

"I don't mind. In fact I think it will be fun. Vanessa is an interesting person, but I've never met Gary."

"He's from Tulsa. The Chief hired him when we needed someone with more sophisticated computer skills to help out in the department. We usually work the night shift together since we're the new guys."

"How does he like Mesa? This is a pretty small town, especially compared to a city like Tulsa."

"Actually he likes it pretty well. He thinks the people are friendly, and he even likes the climate. What he didn't like was the lack of eligible women. That's why he's so excited about tonight."

Shea had always found it easy to talk to David, and the trip to Alpine went very quickly. Shea had never been to Giuseppe's, which was considered one of the finest restaurants in the region. Located on a four-acre lot on the edge of town, it boasted breathtaking views of mountains during the day and a panoramic image of city lights at night. Inside the restaurant Gary and Vanessa were sitting in the waiting area, talking and holding drinks. Vanessa was wearing a short lace burgundy skirt that showed off her long slender legs and a burgundy satin tank top that emphasized her toned body. She looked stunning.

"You look very glamorous for a first-time mom," said Vanessa giving Shea a hug.

"You look wonderful," said Shea, returning the compliment.

"I think our table is ready," said Gary who had just caught the hostess' eye. "Let's go in."

As soon as they were seated at a table next to a sweeping window draped with twinkling lights, Gary ordered a bottle of merlot. They spent a few minutes deciding on appetizers, Giuseppe's Quesadillas, and a few minutes more choosing entrees, shrimp scampi, veal, lasagna, and Fettuccine Alfredo. Finally they managed to get into the subject about which everyone was thinking.

"How's the murder investigation going?" asked Vanessa bluntly. "Or can you not talk about that?"

"We can tell you that it's proceeding," said Gary. "We are following all possible leads."

"In other words, the usual official line," said David.

"Which very politely means none of your business," said Vanessa good-naturedly. "David I'm not surprised that you became a policeman. I knew when you went into the army that you were just trying to avoid your fate."

"Did you guys know that Vanessa was a double homecoming queen?" David asked, quickly and deftly changing the subject. "When she was a high school senior at Mesa High, she was the homecoming queen. She went straight into college at Mesa State and became homecoming queen again when she was a senior."

"Really?" said Gary, obviously impressed.

"Did you know that David made the state finals for track in the 1,500 meter race when he was a senior," said Vanessa in an attempt to turn the tables. "Of course I had already graduated two years earlier, but everyone in town was very excited that a hometown boy was doing so well. He came in first that year. We all thought he would go to college on one of the track scholarships he was offered, but David surprised everyone by enlisting in the military."

"It was the right thing to do at the time," said David.

Vanessa and David exchanged a look of understanding. Obviously they both knew why David had enlisted. It was just as obvious to Shea that David didn't want to discuss it right now.

"How about you Gary?" she asked to turn unwanted attention away from her date. "Were you into athletics?"

"I played football at Tulsa State University. Running back. And I played for the Oklahoma Sooners for a season until I hurt my knee."

"Really?" asked Shea, wondering if her grandmother had ever seen Gary play on televison. Vanessa just smiled. Professional athletes didn't impress her.

"Did you ever play baseball?" asked David.

"Sure as a kid. And later with my college buddies. Why?"

"Because there are a lot of kids around here who could use some Little League coaches. I was thinking of volunteering, and I'm going to recruit some of the other guys at the station."

Shea tried to imagine Aaron Kominski coaching pre-teens. The image just wouldn't compute. "Will you have girls on the teams?"

"You bet. The teams can be single-sex or coed, whatever the

players want."

After a dessert of tiramisu and espresso, David and Shea said they had to leave.

"I was wondering if you would like to go to the Blue Note Club," said Gary to Vanessa. "They're having a jazz group tonight."

"I love jazz."

David, who had told Shea the story of the infamous singles ad, smiled at her. When they parted from the other couple in the parking lot, Shea whispered to him, "It looks like they're hitting it off."

"Yeah. I hope it takes. Gary has been a lonely guy," said David.

Shea thought the same could be said of her escort.

On the return trip to Mesa, they listened to the radio and discovered they both liked Garth Brooks and Toby Keith. David was rather noncommittal on the Backstreet Boys while Shea definitely rejected the musical talents of the Spice Girls. In comparing their literary preferences, Shea admitted she was addicted to murder mysteries, especially Agatha Christie. David said he had every Tony Hillerman book ever written. They agreed to disagree on the best movie of the century, with Shea holding out for Casablanca and David opting for The Godfather.

When they arrived at Shea's house, David stood by the car while Shea opened the front door with her key. Upstairs a light shone in Mary's window, signaling that the nurse's aide was simultaneously watching both the television and the baby.

"Thanks for the evening. It was good to get out," said Shea as she started to enter the corridor.

"My pleasure."

David opened the door to his jeep.

"David, just one thing. I don't know if it's important, but I thought I would just pass along a piece of gossip."

Shea repeated the conversation she had recently held with Opal. "She said that she told this guy, 'I never date married men or wife beaters'. Do you think it means anything?"

"It might. I'll certainly keep it in the back of my mind."

"Good night, then."

Upstairs Shea told Mary that she had returned and that she was too wired up from the late-night espresso to go right to sleep.

"I'll just take forty winks then. Wake me up when your program is over, and you're ready to go to bed."

Shea hung up her new dress, uncertain when she would have an occasion to wear it again, stripped off her nylons, and changed gratefully into white cotton pajamas. Feeling infinitely more comfortable, she checked on the baby, who was sleeping soundly, and then turned on the monitor in her own bedroom. From across the hall, she could hear Mary softly snoring which made her smile. The woman could be asleep in an instant and be completely alert in the same amount of time.

Settling on goose down pillows on her bed, Shea reached for the remote and clicked on the television.

"Tonight's program is about an insurance scam, industrial vandalism for profit and gain . . . "

Her pleasure in watching the program was interrupted by a ringing telephone. Touching the mute button on the remote, she picked up the telephone, expecting it to be a wrong number.

"Shea?"

It was the same slurred voice, the same tentative tone. Shea tensed, fully alert.

"Marlene, is that you? If it's you Marlene, you have to come back to Mesa. Berta has been attacked. It happened on the same night that you left. You have to come back and tell the police whatever you know."

Shea spoke rapidly before the caller could hang up. In the background, she could hear tinkling glass, loud music, and talkative people. She wondered if Marlene might be calling from a casino or a bar.

"Berta's been hurt? Did he do that? Did he go back and hurt her?"

"Marlene," said Shea in a firm voice. "What do you know? Who are you talking about?"

"I should never have told him about the lottery ticket," said the sobbing woman at the other end of the line.

Before Shea could answer, Marlene hung up. Quickly Shea dialed David's number at his apartment, but as usual the phone just rang.

"When is this guy going to get an answering machine?" she said impatiently to no one in particular. She then dialed the station house.

"Helen, do you know how I can reached David?" she asked when the dispatcher answered.

"No, dear. He's not in a police cruiser so I can't reach him. He must be in his jeep."

"If you hear from him, please tell him to call me. I've had another message from Marlene."

Shea turned on the program again. Then it hit her.

Damn, I've been stupid, she thought. We've all been stupid.

At that moment, David was sitting across town in front of the liquor store on University Avenue. Tonight was a perfect night to stake out the telephone box, he thought, because as an off-duty cop, he could drive his own car and very civilian clothes, such as the jeans, tee-shirt and light jacket he now wore. He only hoped that he wouldn't be too conspicuous since he intended to stay there until the store closed.

It was a long shot, but it paid off. At one in the morning, a man approached the phone box. There were few customers around, because the place was ready to close. He stood next to the box, nervously smoking a cigarette and eyeing the young college girls who were leaving the store. They didn't even bother to glance at him. To them, he seemed like any other smelly, dirty transient.

Fifteen minutes later, the telephone rang, and the man picked it up. He listened intensely, spoke in the receiver briefly and hung up the telephone. Without bothering to check if anyone was following him, he began to walk north on University Avenue.

David waited until the man was a block away, and then he started his jeep. He hoped he could follow at a pace that would not alert the guy, who seemed oblivious to any activity around him. For several blocks he followed the man until he entered the building, the Franciscan Hotel.

Shea was right, David thought as he drove past without stopping. It was good information.

Giuseppe's Quesadillas

6 corn tortillas   ½ pound shredded cheese
1 long green chile

1. Under a broiler, toast the chile until the skin can be peeled. Cut into 6 long strips.
2. Soften tortillas in a microwave or on top of a griddle.
3. Place cheese and green chiles on top of 3 tortillas. Cover each with another tortilla.
4. Warm in oven at 350 degrees until cheese melts.

*For a variation on this recipe, flour tortillas and any additional topping can be substituted. Quesadillas can also be lightly fried in vegetable oil until cheese melts.

La Mesa Noticia, Wednesday, June 12

The Town Calendar

The Globe Theatre on Main Street is holding a "World War II Film Festival" this week. Each day the theatre will feature a classic film. Monday's film is "Casablanca." Admission is free for all who surfed in World War II.

Mesa Medical Clinic is sponsoring a blood drive to replenish their supplies. Contributors with A, B, O or any other letter of the alphabet are needed.

Immaculate Conception Church is planning a bazaar to be held on the feast of Corpus Christi. Father Romero says that all those who didn't volunteer last year should do so this year. Confession will be held today at 6:00 p.m.

(Editor's Note: Tuesday's Letter to the Editor should have read "Why are the *roads* so bad around here?")

CHAPTER NINE

"David," said the Chief who had walked in just as the patrolman was finishing his shift, "we've got to bring in those girls."

David groaned inwardly. He had been dreading this. Yet he knew the Chief was right. They were going to have to question Rosie and Ceci De Anda again. And this time it wouldn't be so gentle. They needed some answers.

"Who do you want first?" he asked.

"Isn't Rosie working the first shift this morning?"

"Yes, sir." David had just checked with the Roadhouse to see who was waitressing.

"Then bring in her sister."

Twenty minutes later, David arrived at the De Anda home. When Ceci answered the doorbell, she didn't give him her usual cheery smile. Instead she stood looking glum and anxious.

"Ceci, I need you to come downtown with me," David said as kindly as he could.

She hesitated, glancing sideways at him with suspicion in her eyes. "I've got to call my neighbor to come stay with my Mom. It'll take a few minutes."

David waited in the kitchen while Ceci made the telephone call. In a few minutes, a woman, approximately thirty-years-old, came into the house holding a four-year-old boy by the hand. He immediately went to the television and turned on Sesame Street. Since they seemed to be at ease in the De Anda home, David assumed they must be accustomed to helping out the girls.

"Thanks so much, Mrs. Hadley," said Ceci, obviously embarrassed to be escorted from her home by a policeman.

"It's no problem, Ceci," said the lady, looking at David curiously. "We're always happy to help."

"Can you tell me what this is about, David?" asked Ceci as she was getting into the car. She had always liked David, but until now, she had never feared him.

"We just have a few more questions, Ceci," he replied. Despite himself, he felt sorry for her. He hated to put her and her sister through this, and he really believed they had nothing to do with the murder. But instinct and common sense told him that they knew something, that they were holding something back. With that in mind, he drove in silence, deliberately allowing the young girl to feel the discomfort.

At the station house, he took Ceci into the interrogation room where Kominski was waiting.

"Good morning," Aaron said with surprising courtesy. "Would you like some coffee?"

David stared at him. Kominski had never displayed such social grace before. Perhaps it was because Ceci was an especially pretty girl. Perhaps he had a plan.

Ceci shook her head.

"Okay, I need to hear again about the day of the funeral. You went to the reception, right?"

Ceci nodded her head this time.

"Tell me what you did there."

"We talked to some people, and we had some cookies. And, uh, I needed to go to the bathroom, so we went upstairs."

"That's when you looked around?" Kominski's voice was still gentle.

"Yes, I looked in some of the bedrooms. I had never been in the O'Daniels' home before. I wanted to see what it looked like."

"And just what were you looking for?"

"I don't understand," began Ceci in a faltering voice.

"Like hell you don't," Kominski thundered so loud that even David almost jumped. "You were looking for something that Marlene told you about. Tell me what you were looking for."

"We heard, Marlene told us, we thought . . . " Ceci couldn't seem to complete the sentence.

"You thought there was something valuable in the house, didn't you?"

"Yes." Her voice was a whisper.

"So you and Rosie stole a key so that you could return later and search the house when it was empty."

"No, Rosie didn't do anything. She didn't know anything about the key. She didn't take it. I did." Ceci stopped and put her hands over her mouth to stop her lips from trembling. "I found it in the kitchen drawer when I was looking for a towel to clean up a mess."

"Then you returned later and hit Berta over the head, sending her to the hospital."

"No!"

134

She spat out the word so emphatically that David believed her.

"No, I didn't attack Berta. I've known her for years. She knows my Mom."

"So where were you at twelve-thirty that night?"

"I've already told you, I was working at the restaurant."

"Ceci," David interrupted, "you weren't working at that hour. You closed the restaurant early that evening, because there were so few customers. I talked to Hester Fernshaw. She says that everyone left before midnight."

Ceci seemed to crumble. "I didn't want Rosie to know. She doesn't like it when I go there."

"Where were you?" demanded Kominski.

"I went out to the river levee to see if I could find any of my crowd. I drove around awhile, but I didn't see any of my friends. So I came home."

"What time did you get home?"

Ceci looked miserable. "About one in the morning."

"Did anyone see you come in?"

"No, I went straight to my room."

"So you don't know if Rosie was in bed or not?"

"I assumed she was."

"Did you see her car?" asked David, referring to their mother's old Chevrolet that Rosie sometimes drove.

"No. It's always locked in the garage. I parked mine on the street. This morning it was gone, and the garage door was open. She had already left for work."

"What were you going to do with the key, Ceci? Steal something from the O'Daniels home?" asked David, determined to try a different tactic.

"I don't know. It's just that Marlene kept talking about a lottery ticket. She said that Dorothy hadn't signed it before she died. That meant that anyone could turn it in and claim the money. And it didn't seem that Shea knew anything about it. Everyone said she was so worried about how to pay the bills and all. So I thought, if I could find it, well, possession is nine-tenths of the law, right? I wouldn't be hurting her, because she wouldn't know anything about it."

"No, Ceci. It would still be stealing," explained David patiently. He looked at Kominski who just shrugged as if to say, what can you expect. "So where's the key?"

"I don't know. When I got home, I looked for it. It wasn't in my purse."

Kominski motioned for David to follow him from the room. When they were outside in the hallway, he said, "Call Gary. Have him come down here to give a polygraph test. I'll go back inside and get her to agree to take one. Then pick up Rosie De Anda."

David called Gary who said he would be down in fifteen minutes. Afterwards he went to pick up Rosie at the Mesa Roadhouse in his police cruiser. Inside the restaurant, he saw Rosie standing at a cash register, looking as if she were about to pick up the telephone. The place was empty of customers except for one man who stood at the counter, holding Hester Fernshaw by the arm.

"Just get out of here, Willie," she pleaded. "You've already cost Curtis his job here. Don't make me lose mine."

"I need some money, woman, or you know what I'll do."

"I think you'd better let go of her," said David. He had entered the dining area quietly without attracting the man's attention.

Willie Fernshaw looked behind him to see the six foot plus officer standing behind him. David had his hands looped casually through his holster belt, a fact which did not escape Willie's attention.

"Of course, officer," he said silkily. "I'm a peaceful man." He relinquished Hester's arm and climbed off the stool. "I was just having a little disagreement with my wife."

"Hester, are you okay?" asked David.

"I'm fine. Thanks, David."

"I don't want to see you around here threatening Hester again," said David.

Willie, who sported a three-day-old beard and bad breath, was smirking as he left the restaurant.

"What was that about?"

"He's been back for awhile, because he ran out of money. He kept hanging around here, and the girls kept coming up short in the cash register. When they finally told Leland, he blamed Curtis and fired him. He thinks all teenagers are shoplifters and pilferers."

"I told Mr. Johannson that I didn't think it was Curtis, David, but he didn't believe me," said Rosie. Sensing that David wanted to talk to her alone, she said, "Hester, we'll be outside."

David held the door while Rosie, who was wearing her waitressing outfit, a pale blue blouse and skirt, walked to the front parking lot.

"Rosie, we've got Ceci down at the station," David said in lowered tones so that a passing customer couldn't hear. Rosie stood silently, tense and alert. "And we need you to come, too."

"I thought that was why you were here." Opening the door, she called out, "Hester, can you manage alone awhile?"

"Sure thing, Rosie."

136

Without another word, Rosie got into the front seat of the police cruiser. "Is she okay?"

"She was when I left. She's pretty shaken up. That's all I can tell you now, Rosie."

When they arrived at the red brick three-story building on Forrest Lane, which served as combination police quarters and lawyers' offices, David took Rosie into the same room where Ceci had been earlier. Hank Hatfield, a regular customer at the Roadhouse, smiled at her but looked away when she didn't return the greeting. David knew that he understood why she was not feeling very friendly today.

"Aaron," David said as soon as he entered the room, "this is Rosie De Anda. Rosie, this is Aaron Kominski, our investigator."

Kominski took one look at the young woman and realized that this was a strong adversary. He quickly decided that he would waste his time by playing any mind games, so he came straight to the point.

"When did you learn about the lottery ticket?"

"Marlene told me," said Rosie.

"When did she tell you?"

"The same night that Dorothy told her."

"That was the night that Dorothy was killed. How did she tell you? On the phone? In person? Damn it, girl, this is like pulling teeth!" Aaron shouted.

In his usual corner, David watched carefully. He knew that Aaron was employing a tactic as usual, but he couldn't help feeling some concern for Rosie. Rosie, however, was perfectly calm and collected.

"Marlene asked me to give her a ride home that night. So I went to the restaurant and picked her up. She was so excited she couldn't wait to tell someone that Dorothy thought she had a winning lottery ticket worth millions."

"Well, we're finally getting somewhere. Do you know if she told anyone else?"

"I think she told Bob. They're pretty tight."

"Did you tell anyone?"

"When I got home, I told Ceci. She was very excited."

"How long did it take you to drop Marlene off and make it to your house?"

Rosie hesitated, looking at David.

"It takes about twenty minutes, doesn't it Rosie?" David answered for her.

"And from your house to the restaurant, it would take only ten

137

minutes, correct," said Kominski, who had already calculated the distance.

"Yes," said Rosie. Her composure had disintegrated, and she was now close to tears.

"So which one of you went back to shoot Dorothy? Or were you in it together?"

When Rosie didn't reply, Kominski continued, "We have convinced Ceci to take a polygraph test, so you don't want to give us any false information. What's the problem? Are you protecting your sister?"

"I won't answer, and I won't take a polygraph test. You can't force me to do that. I know my rights. Ceci may not know that, but I do."

"Ceci's already told us that she stole the key from the O'Daniels' home. Which one of you went back and attacked her? Did both of you go? Did you think you were going to find the lottery ticket?"

At that moment, the door opened, and Gary handed a long sheet to Kominski. It contained the jagged lines which even at a distance designated the form as a polygraph test.

"Well, this is very interesting," said Kominski in an exaggerated tone. "According to this test, your sister has just admitted that she shot Dorothy O'Daniels, and that she broke into her home. Looks like it's all over."

"That's a lie," screamed Rosie, jumping to her feet and pounding on the table. "It's not true. I did it. I'll sign a confession. Right now."

Kominski handed her the paper.

"This isn't Ceci's test. It has someone else's name on it," said Rosie.

"You got it," said Kominski. "By the way, that lottery ticket. It was a dud. Not worth a tinker's damn. David, read her her rights."

On Wednesday morning, Shea had showered and dressed, ready to leave for the hospital, after only a few hours sleep. She had simply been too excited. It took her more time to choose just the right outfit, the perfect receiving blanket, and matching booties for the baby than it did to dress herself. After convincing George that they could get breakfast at a MacDonald's drive-through, they arrived at the hospital with time to spare before Dr. MacKenzie made her rounds.

"Do I need to take care of any business?" she asked the nurse.

"I think you have to sign some forms down in the business office. It's right next to the emergency room."

"Thanks."

Shea took the stairs which opened onto the emergency room which she remembered very well. In one of the cubicles, which had open curtains, she saw Dr. Yadiri examining a fat baby, about six months old, who was crying at the top of her lungs.

"She's going to be okay, Mrs. Lopez," Dr. Yadiri was saying to the baby's mother. "Nurse, could you please translate. Tell her that the baby has an ear infection and needs some antibiotics. I'm going to give her a prescription."

Upon hearing the translation, Mrs. Lopez burst forth with rapid Spanish.

Poor thing, thought Shea, who was shamelessly eavesdropping. She doesn't have any insurance or even Medicaid. And her husband is out of a job. They don't have any money. That was something to which she could relate.

Shea continued to the business office and signed all the necessary forms. A few days ago, the large amounts at the bottom of the page would have sent her into hysterics, but today she did not even have to think about the money. As she walked back to the stairs, she encountered the nurse who had assisted Dr. Yadiri.

"Do you know if that lady was the wife of Hector Lopez?" she asked.

"Yes, that's Lydia Lopez. He's the one who's still in jail for killing that restaurant waitress," said the nurse who didn't recognize Shea. "It's a shame for her, all alone with three small children."

"Yes, it is," agreed Shea.

Upstairs she received the release papers from Mark's nurse. She was stuffing the papers into the diaper bag when she heard, "Hello, Shea."

Vanessa Williams, followed by three incredibly young-looking interns, was entering the room. Shea thought they looked as if they belonged in a junior high study hall rather than a hospital. Baby docs, she had heard the nurses call them.

"Good morning, Vanessa. Is it really okay if I take him home?"

"He's all yours. But I want to see him in my office in one week. And if you have any problems, you should telephone me day or night."

After Vanessa and her entourage left, a nurse's aide and a candy striper descended upon them. While the attendants fussed over Mark and brought them complimentary boxes of diapers and formula, Shea couldn't help but notice the difference between her treatment and the situation for Hector Lopez' wife. When the baby was dressed, she placed him in the state-of-the-art stroller which she had ordered just yesterday. The stroller had a bottom shelf which most mothers used for shopping packages. Mark's stroller would hold the portable oxygen tank which he would need on the drive home.

"Okay, kiddo, I brought the truck around to the front of the hospital. That security guard gave me heck, but when I said it was for your baby, he said I could have a few minutes," said George, who stomped into the room like an invading army who was rescuing hostages. Without further ceremony, he swept up several items, including diapers, formula, and flower vases, and strode through the door.

I guess he wants to make a getaway while we can, thought Shea with amusement. George hated hospitals and distrusted all doctors.

Downstairs, George placed Mark in the car seat with the oxygen tank on the floor. He loaded the truck bed with all his paraphernalia.

"This going-home business requires almost as much preparation as the invasion of Normandy," grumbled George, who had been a very young private in that battle.

Silently Shea agreed. Everything had been a little stressful. When they arrived home, however, she relaxed as soon as she placed the baby into his hooded crib, fastened the breathing canula on his nose, and placed the oxygen monitor on his toe. She had decorated the room with Beatrix Potter curtains and linens and had purchased music boxes with soothing lullabies. One of them she now put to immediate use.

Immediately Mark, who had been somewhat restless on the drive home, went back to sleep, leaving Shea with little to do except deposit herself in the antique oak rocking chair and stare at him. It seemed as if she could do that all day. While she watched her sleeping infant, who looked both vulnerable and peaceful at the same time, the face of Lydia Lopez kept intruding. She was haunted by the thin body of the young woman and her gaunt eyes. Obviously the past several days had taken their toll on her.

Everyone has said that they believe he is not guilty, she thought. If that's the case, then he shouldn't be in jail when his family needs him, she thought.

Picking up the cordless telephone which she had brought from her bedroom, she dialed a number.

"Mr. Tyler, please," she said to the receptionist. "Jason, this is Shea." In her excitement, she didn't realize that she had used his Christian name. And he didn't correct her. "I have a predicament, and I think you can help me with it."

After waiting for his response, she began to explain the circumstances. "What can we do? Is that all? How soon do you think? Okay, I'll call him right now. I'll wait to hear from you. Yes, the baby is just fine. We're all settled in. Thanks, Jason."

Shea pressed the "off" button and then pressed "on" immediately. She dialed another number. There was no answer. She tried a third number.

"Hello, could I speak to Officer De Vargas? Thank you," said Shea to Francine, the morning dispatcher.

"David, this is Shea."

"Shea," said David. "I was just about to call you about something?"

"Should I go first?"

"Why don't I come over there? I could bring something for lunch. Did you pick up the baby?"

"Yes to all of the above."

David slammed down the telephone and headed for the door. Since he was helping with the investigation during his off-duty hours, he could take as long a lunch break as he wanted.

"Chief," he said rapping on Beau's door. Because Beau's door was always ajar, this was a pro forma gesture.

"So how did the interrogations go?"

"Not too well. Both girls are admitting to everything except shooting John F. Kennedy. Too young for that."

"Yeah, I figured. They're pretty scared now. Especially since each one wants to protect the other."

"That's what I thought. So can you convince Kominski not to book Rosie right now? She has refused to take a polygraph test. So did Ceci."

"Yeah, we couldn't use that confession anyway. A good lawyer would tear us to shreds. Confession under duress, obtained by a fake polygraph test. And anyway, Rosie's lying, because she thinks she's protecting Ceci."

"What are they hiding? Do you think they're guilty?"

"They're guilty of something, son."

"I think Hector Lopez should be released from jail. He didn't know anything about that lottery ticket. Gary gave him a polygraph test, and he came up clean. Besides his family needs him."

"I agree with you, David, but I'm not the judge. You'd be better off talking to a good lawyer. Judge Ayes is likely to rebond him, but it'll be at a stiff price. Do you have that kind of money?"

"As a matter of fact, I don't," said David and left to pick up pizzas. He had ordered two from Luna's Pharmacy. In addition to serving as a drugstore and pharmacy, the mom and pop business also had a real old-fashioned soda fountain which served delicious pastrami sandwiches, mouth-watering french fries, and pizza which was equal to any sold in Austin, Texas.

When he arrived at the O'Daniels Homestead, the front door was thrown open, and Shea flew down the steps.

"I could smell the pizza when you turned the corner. Please tell me one of those is Canadian Bacon?"

"I don't think they know what Canadian Bacon is in this town, but one of them is pepperoni. And it's to die for," he said in a mocking tone.

"So I've heard. Do you mind if we eat upstairs? I don't want to leave the baby alone even for a moment."

In the nursery, Shea had placed a pitcher of iced tea and plates. After rolling in the office chair from the study for David, she took the rocker again.

"Pizza?" asked George as he strolled in and grabbed a slice of sausage pizza. He walked over to the crib, made a face at the sleeping infant, and left.

"Has he had that goofy smile on his face all day?" asked David.

"It gets worse," Shea told him. "He talks to the baby. In baby talk."

David smiled and then got down to business. "Shea, I brought the pizzas to bribe you. I really need a favor."

"Sure."

"Chief Cummings thinks that Hector Lopez could be released on bail again, but there are some conditions. First, the bail is going to be higher than last time. And I don't think Leland Johannson is going to post bail twice. Second, Hector will need some employment. He can't go back to the restaurant."

"Hmm," said Shea. "And you think since I'm rolling in dough, that I can handle all this?"

"Well, I just thought it might be a real nice thing . . ."

"Done," said Shea.

"Do you mean . . .?"

"Done. Jason Tyler is taking care of this right now, speaking to Jessica Gutierrez, who is going to talk to Judge Ayes, who will be very disposed to grant release to Hector, because he has been offered gainful employment as a gardener at the Alpine Country Club of which Jason Tyler is a prominent member. Furthermore, an anonymous client of Mr. Tyler's, who shall remain nameless, has offered to post any bail which the judge sees fit to set. And finally, Johannson's Market is, as we speak, delivering groceries, diapers, and milk to the Lopez family in the Mesa Trailer Park. And Luna's Pharmacy will deliver all medications prescribed by Dr. Yadiri to the same."

"You did all that this morning?"

"It was a good day."

"I'll say. Cute kid," said David, looking at Mark and casually biting into a slice of pizza. "Does he take after his dad?"

When Mary came home from the hospital at dinner time, she found George in the kitchen taking wrapped packages out of a paper bag that looked and certainly smelled like gorditas.

"From Jorge's Diner," he explained. "We're livin' on take-out now. This place is just revolvin' around that little brat upstairs."

"Where's Shea?" asked Mary, not a bit fooled by his umbrage. If a seventy-four year old man could glow, then George was glowing.

"Upstairs."

Knowing that Shea would be in the nursery, Mary crept softly up the stairs and into the baby's room. Curled up in the rocker with a Beatrix Potter afghan thrown over her, Shea slept soundlessly. In his crib, Mark was also sleeping, his tiny nose covered with the life-giving canula. The room smelled of talcum powder and sweet baby formula.

Just as it should, thought Mary with satisfaction.

Returning to the hallway, she noticed a lump on the daybed in the study. Peering in, she saw that it was David, stretched out in a dead heap.

"It looks like it's just you and me," she told George in the kitchen. "Should we wake them?"

"Nah. When it's time for his shift, I'll just throw him out the window."

While they were enjoying the gorditas and freshly-brewed tea, David came into the kitchen, looking slightly rumpled and more than slightly sheepish.

"Are we goin' to have to start chargin' you room and board, boy?" asked George.

"No, sir, I'm on my way."

"You'll be having some dinner now, won't you?" asked Mary.

"Thank you, but I really don't have time. I've got to go home and shower, and then I have to make a stop before I take my shift."

"Such a nice, polite young man," said Mary as David left through the back door.

George gave her a piercing look. "That boy's brain is always turnin'. Wonder what he's up to now?"

❖

"Do you mean I can go home?" asked Hector in disbelief as he once again stood to watch Judge Ayes exiting the courtroom. There were no spectators, because it had been a hastily-assembled hearing.

"Yes, you can," said his lawyer, Jessica Gutierrez. Her soft brown hair hung in wavy curls, the result of birth and not beauty parlor techniques. For the first time since she had been representing her client, she smiled, showing dimples in both cheeks.

"And you can start your new job tomorrow," she continued. "There will be a van coming to the trailer park to take a few of you to work at the Alpine Country Club. You'll like it there. It's very pretty, and the manager is a good man."

She didn't add that someone through Jason Tyler had offered to pay her fees for this case which she had declined. It was her responsibility, she firmly told Jason.

"How did all this happen?" Hector asked his lawyer.

"I'm not at liberty to say," said Jessica, who had been racking her own brain trying to figure out the identity of the anonymous client. "Just accept is as a good-will gesture."

In the corridor, Hector saw his young wife waiting for him. She had none of the children with her which meant that a neighbor must be watching the two boys and the ailing baby.

"Comesta Felipa?" Hector asked immediately about the baby.

"Esta bien," said Lydia. She was crying again, but this time she was smiling. "Hector tenemos comida a la casa. Mucha comida."

"Gracias a Dios," he murmured. Wherever the job and the food were coming from, he really didn't care at this point. He was just grateful.

"Yes, he was here that night," said the security officer, a young man approximately two or three years younger than David.

He had told David that he had just finished a security-officers' training course a few months ago in San Antonio and had been hired by Leland Johannson. He brushed back his sandy blonde hair as he struggled to recall the details. "I check in on Mr. Johannson every night. I saw him sitting in his office, working on reports."

"Did you speak to him? Did he see you?"

"No, he doesn't like to be disturbed."

David's next stop also yielded no results, and he arrived at the police station somewhat out of sorts. His trip to the Alpine Airport had been a fruitless quest for information which had come up empty. Leland Johannson had flown to Midland on the night in question, just as he had stated. He had even filed a flight plan.

Which virtually eliminated him as a suspect, thought David, for both incidents. That took him back to the waitresses and the older cook.

No matter how good-natured he seemed, Bob Crockett's police record revealed that he did have a temper and could lash out at someone in a momentary loss of self-control. Furthermore, he was a big man as well as strong. Despite his overweight, he looked like he worked out occasionally with bar bells. And he had a lifestyle that was a little beyond the means of a restaurant cook. David knew that the Harley-Davidson he drove was one of the most expensive models around. He also had that cabin up at Silver Lake and a nice motorboat as well. Like many others in the area, Bob owned more than a few guns. According to his own admission, his Smith and Wesson had been stolen. Perhaps he had another one that was unregistered? That had been known to occur.

The question was, did he need money badly enough to shoot Dorothy O'Daniels for a lottery ticket? Did Marlene call him when she reached her house? Did he return to the O'Daniels' home and bash Bertha over the head?

Then there was Marlene. True, Dorothy and Marlene, who was twenty years her junior, had been very chummy ever since Marlene came to work for the restaurant about six years ago. They had gone weekly to the bingo parlor and went to the movies at least once a month. Unlike Dorothy, however, who by all accounts had been very conservative with her money, it seemed that Marlene might have a gambling problem. Shea had told him about the telephone conversation with her mother, and it seemed to fit. Marlene always took her vacations outside of town and rarely talked about them. Perhaps she had been gambling and losing money for some time. That would mean that she was in dire need of money. Did she take off. because she was frightened of what she had done? Or was she frightened of someone else? Why hadn't she called again?

Once more he had to wonder if she had the nerves of steel to pull off cold-blooded murder. Why not? Her concern for Dorothy and her grandchild might be just an act. No one in town seemed to know much about her. David knew that she had lived in Amarillo before she came to Mesa. He thought he might give the Amarillo police a call tonight.

Finally there were the two girls. It was very likely that both of them knew within minutes of Marlene entering the car with Rosie that there was a lottery winner who was worth millions. They also knew from Marlene that Dorothy had not yet signed the ticket. So time was a critical factor. Neither of them had ever been in trouble before, but that didn't necessarily eliminate them as suspects. Ceci had lied on two counts. First, she had not been in the restaurant as she had said at the time of Berta's attack. Second, she had lied, or at least omitted the fact, that she had taken Dorothy's key.

Rosie, despite her passionate confession, also was covering up something. She was the second person to know about the lottery ticket. Perhaps she had a revolver. Lots of women who worked or were out late at night carried one. Very often they bought or borrowed one from a friend without bothering to get the proper registration papers. She could have returned to the restaurant and killed Dorothy. It could have even been unintentional, not premeditated. It was possible that she meant only to stun the older woman. And not being a good shot, postulated David, she fatally injured her instead. Maybe she made the confession in a calculated move, knowing that the police would think she was covering up for her sister.

It was going to take more than interrogations and even polygraph tests to uncover the truth. Because the police simply weren't asking the right questions. David decided to act on one more hunch.

"Gary," he said in a much better tone than he had used when he first entered the station house, "can you get me some telephone records?"

"You're going to need a court order from Judge Ayes. Once

you have the warrant, I can get them for you real easy."

"Okay," said David, picking up the telephone. He sure hoped the judge was still up at this hour.

"Mary, why don't you take a nap for a few hours? I'll stay up until twelve. There's a program I've been watching late at night, and I'm kind of hooked. I'll put Mark in the cradle in my bedroom."

Shea was trying to convince Mary to rest awhile, because she did look tired. Fortunately Mary was one of those people who could rest in three or four hour intervals, and then be perfectly fine. Shea really envied that asset.

"I think I will. Isn't it grand that I don't have to go into the hospital anymore? I can putter around here all day tomorrow? I was thinking about making some Irish soda bread."

"I would really love that," said Shea.

In Mary's own words, it had really been "grand" to have her around. She brought a spirit of optimism and hope to the household. Shea knew that if Berta were there with her, no matter that she was uncommonly fond of the woman, they would both be grieving even more for her grandmother. While Mary certainly felt sincere sympathy for Shea and George, she hadn't known Dorothy O'Daniels. Her lack of personal involvement was something of a balm.

Somehow Shea felt her grandmother approved. There were so many times that she could feel her presence as strongly as that of her late husband. Dorothy Joe's spirit, however, exhibited the same sort of maternal care than she had exhibited when she was alive. Shea truly expected at any moment to feel Joe's hand on her shoulder or to smell the scent of her lilac cologne. She could imagine her grandmother bending over the cradle where Mark now slept, still hooked up to his oxygen machine, and touching his cheek.

Feeling more calm than she had in months, Shea picked up the remote and turned on the television. She had finally gotten cable installed in her bedroom and Mary's. So she could comfortably watch television in her bed while she kept an eye on Mark.

"Tonight's episode of 'White Collar Crime' is about a brilliant young man in Singapore who tapped into a computer program and . . ."

Shea settled under the covers to watch what was fast becoming her favorite program.

Jorge's Gorditas

1 lb. ground beeef	2 lb. cornmeal
2 large potatoes, diced and cooked	1 t salt
½ lb. cheddar cheese	t baking powder
1 medium diced tomato	1 diced clove garlic
1 medium diced onion	1 cup sliced tomato
1 cup shortening	salt & pepper to taste

1. Mix the cornmeal, baking powder and salt with water. Knead and make small patties.
2. Fry patties in hot shortening. Remove and cool.
3. Partially fry meat. Add salt, pepper, garlic, onion, and potatoes. Fry until tender.
4. Slice open patties. Fill with meat mixture.
5. Garnish with tomatoes, lettuce, and cheese.

La Mesa Noticia, June 15

Personal and Want Ads

Softball practice for eight to ten-year-olds will be held Saturday from 10 a.m. to 12 p.m. at the Mesa City Park. The Junior Cardinals will meet on the south field, and the Junior Astros will meet on the north field.

The Irish-American Society will hold its monthly meeting on Tuesday night at 6 p.m. in the home of Orlando Pavarotti.

Typesetter wanted. Contact La Mesa Noticia.

My duck is missing again. Anyone seeing my duck, please call 555-6613. Manuel Escodero.

(Editor's Note: Yesterday's editorial should have read *ball* instead of *bull*.)

CHAPTER TEN

At 1:15 a.m. Shea's telephone rang again. Grabbing it immediately, she answered expectantly, "David?"

"No, Shea, it's Vanessa. Gary just dropped me off at my apartment. He had a call on his cellular telephone while we were returning here that there is a fire at the Mesa Roadhouse!"

Thanking for friend for the news, Shea dropped the telephone and ran across the hallway to wake Mary.

"Have you been awake all this time, Shea?" asked the woman, rising from her bed to look at the clock on her nightstand.

"Yes, but I've got to go out. The restaurant is on fire, and I've got to see if any of the people there have been hurt."

"I'll be right here. You go do what you must."

"Changing quickly into jeans and a white cotton shirt, Shea grabbed the keys to the Mustang and her cellular telephone before running down the stairs to the car. On the way to the restaurant, she tried calling David at home again. When she received no answer, she was sure he was at the fire. It took her only minutes to reach the restaurant on the Highway.

The county fire department was already on the scene with two fire trucks and several people manning hoses. Others walked around assessing the damage. On the perimeter of the fire scene, she saw David standing with Aaron Kominski and Beau Cummings. Beau was talking into a cell phone. Shea walked over within hearing distance behind the three police officers.

"All right. I'll be right there." Beau turned to the other two men. "Jaime has picked up Willie Fernshaw. He was only a few blocks away, trying to get to a car he had stashed by the frontage road."

"Damn, if he hadn't given me the slip after he went into that hotel, I could have stopped him before he did this," said David.

"You did your best. Whoever gave you the tip that he was back in town to do a job for someone sure did us a favor. If you hadn't been following him tonight, we might never have caught up with him," said Beau.

149

"Those telephone calls he was getting were all from the same person?" asked Kominski.

"Yes," said David. "And now we know why."

"You two get over there and bring him in for questioning. I'm going to the police station and help Jaime and Gary interrogate this guy. If he wants to save himself some trouble, he'll start talking," said Beau. "What the hell are you doing here, young lady?"

Whirling around, the police chief confronted Shea who thought they hadn't noticed her. She knew his gruff tone was only out of concern for her.

"I heard that there was a fire. I wanted to see if anyone was hurt. Did everyone get out?"

"Yes," said David. "The restaurant closed early. No one was around."

"It was never about the lottery ticket, was it?"

"No, Shea. I'm afraid that it wasn't. But you need to go home now. I'll call you later."

Shea watched as Kominski and David left in Kominski's car. For a few more minutes, she sat and watched as the firefighters brought the blaze under control.

It was all about money, she thought. Just from a different source.

As Aaron parked the car in front of the feed and grain, he looked at David for an instance as he checked his model 19 Smith and Wesson. Satisfied, he returned it to his shoulder holster.

"Are you ready?" he asked the younger man.

"Yes, sir," said David, unsnapping the safety lock on his gun holster.

They entered the building through the back door which they knew would be unlocked. As they had expected, the building was deserted except for the security guard who stood within to let them pass. He had been called by Chief Cummings only minutes earlier. The investigator and police officer walked up the flight of stairs to Leland Johannson's office.

Johannson's office was filled with generic metal file cabinets, a couple of plastic molded chairs, and a large metal desk strewn with file folders, papers, overflowing ashtrays, and styrofoam coffee cups. Seated behind the desk in his shirt sleeves and paisley suspenders, the middle-aged man looked up from his paperwork to give the policemen a slightly perturbed look.

"What's happening at the restaurant?" he asked hurriedly before his visitors could speak. "I wanted to go there, but the fire chief said I would just be in the way. Was anyone hurt?"

"No," said Kominski. Against his will, he had to admire the man's poise. He was playing the part of the concerned employer with perfect aplomb. "The restaurant had been closed already. Just like before. Only this time you were more fortunate. There weren't any witnesses around to get rid of."

"I'm afraid I don't know what you mean," said Johannson. He took off his glasses and rubbed his temple as if he had a terrible headache.

"I think you do, Johannson. You tried this before, the night that Dorothy O'Daniels was killed. And you tried it again tonight. Only this time you were successful."

"That's ridiculous. On the night that Dorothy O'Daniels was killed, I was in Midland. You can check the flight plan."

"We did," said David.

"And tonight I've been here all evening trying to balance the budget for three businesses," Leland said with an attempt at indignation. "You can check with the night security officer. Or with the store manager. He came by only half an hour ago."

"I'm sure you have been here all night," said Kominski. He and David had taken positions across from the owner but at opposite ends of the long desk. There was no way that the short, pudgy businessman could race for the door unless he vaulted across the desk. And Kominski doubted he was in any shape to do that.

"I'm positive that you made sure that people saw you here," continued the investigator. In his immaculate, expensive suit with his perfectly groomed hair, the inveswtigator made quite a contrast to the rather rumpled suspect. "That way you would have a good alibi. That's why you hired Willie Fernshaw in the first place. So you didn't have to be present at the restaurant to be responsible for both a murder and arson. You didn't have to be at the O'Daniels home to be responsible for an attack on a maid. You could hire someone for that."

"That's ridi . . . ridiculous," stammered Johannson.

His poise seems to be slipping, thought David.

"We have Willie Fernshaw down at the station. I hear that he's turned his Barbie diary over to the Chief."

"Willie, ah Fernshaw, you say? I don't recognize that name. I don't think he's one of my employees, is he? Oh, now I remember," said Johannson with exaggerated politeness. "His wife works for me, and his son used to work in the restaurant. Unfortunately

I had to let him go when I caught him stealing. Maybe you should look in that direction. This terrible tragedy could have been the work of a disgruntled teenager."

"No," interjected David, angered at the man's lies and slander. "Curtis wasn't stealing. At the same time that his wife went to work for you, Willie came back to town and started hanging around the restaurant, hitting her up for money. If she wouldn't fork out the money, he would take a few dollars at a time from the cash register. You knew it was him, but you fire the son to keep the suspicion off Willie. Every time he screwed up, you had to throw the suspicion on someone else."

"That night in the restaurant when Dorothy told Marlene that she had the lottery ticket, you didn't know anything about it then," said Kominski. "Neither did Willie. It was just a freak accident that Willie, who had a key to the restaurant from you, thought that no one was there when he walked into the place holding a can of gasoline. When Dorothy saw what he was holding, she must have known what was going on. He panicked and shot her with a gun which he probably stole from someone else. Or did you give him a gun?"

Johannson looked at Kominski with hatred in his eyes. He remained silent   .

"Anyway, he had a gun. And when he saw that Dorothy recognized him and knew what he was up to, he panicked and shot her. Then he was so damned scared that he had killed someone that all he could think of doing was to run. He didn't even take the time to steal her watch and ring."

"It was a robbery, everyone knows that," blubbered Johannson. "Her purse was missing."

"We're guessing that he couldn't resist taking Dorothy's purse to see if she had a few extra dollars. And possibly to make it look like a random robbery. He wasn't going to go back to you," said David. "Not after he screwed up the job. And you kept after him to come back and give it a second chance. You were the one who suggested he put the purse and the gun in Hector's trash can to implicate him. Willie would never have thought of that. He didn't even know Hector. You even paid Hector's bail. That way you figured suspicion would fall on him when the restaurant was burned to the ground."

Johannson looked from one man to the other. He couldn't seem to find his voice to say anything.

"Willie got another stroke of luck when his wife got a job in your restaurant. Or did you also plan that?" asked Kominski. "That way it was natural for him to hang around the restaurant a lot. Unfortunately Willie is such a weasel that he couldn't resist trying to wrangle a few extra dollars from his old lady and causing more problems. That was when he heard about the lottery ticket which everyone at the restaurant thought was still in Dorothy's house. He even heard Ceci talking on the telephone to Rosie the night of the funeral reception, telling her that she had stolen the key."

With some surprise, David glanced at Kominski. This was pure conjecture, he knew, because neither of the girls had admitted to anything. But it was a good guess and probably very close to the truth. Probably at the station house, Willie Fernshaw was giving a statement to that effect at this very minute.

"It was no big deal for Willie to steal that key from her purse," said Kominski. "He was the one who went to the house, again thinking it was empty, to look for the ticket. When he found Berta there, he knocked her out, bound her, and then searched the house. But he couldn't find anything."

"He must have been pretty desperate," said David when Kominski paused. "Did he threaten to expose you if you didn't pay him more money? Did you give Marlene money to get out of town so that the police would think it was Bob?"

"I don't know anything about Marlene," said Johannson. "I don't know why she left town. But yes, I was relieved when I heard you were questioning Bob. And Ceci. And Rosie."

He slumped back in his chair, looking defeated.

"That man was out of control," Leland said in biting tones. "I only wanted him to burn down the restaurant so that I could collect the insurance money and save the other businesses. I've had a very bad year. I figured that fires start in restaurant kitchens all the time so it was the best bet. But Willie was an idiot. He killed Dorothy just for a few dollars in her purse. And because he knew she would report him."

Pulling a plain white cotton handkerchief from his pants pocket, Leland wiped his face, which was sweating.

"I told Willie to lay low for awhile, but he wouldn't listen. He never listened. Later when I heard that Berta had been attacked in Dorothy's house, I suspected it was Willie again up to his stupid tricks. I confronted him, and he admitted he had been looking for the lottery ticket. He even offered to share the winnings with me. I told him he was being stupid, that we could never claim the money even if we found the ticket. I ordered him to get out of town for awhile and lay low. But Willie never listened to anyone. He refused to leave and said he would take me down as an accomplice if I tried to go to the police. Finally, to get rid of two problems, I offered to pay him $100,000 if he would set fire to the restaurant and do it right this time."

There was a moment of silence while Leland removed his spectacles and wiped them with the handkerchief. He looked at them critically and put the glasses on the desk. When he spoke, his tone was once again well-modulated and controlled. He looked almost relieved.

"Well, gentlemen, I suppose you now want to take me downtown, as they say. Let me just get my other pair of glasses. These are scratched."

Before Aaron or David could stop him, Leland reached into the desk drawer and pulled out a Colt 45. With one quick movement, he put the pistol to his head and pulled the trigger. When he fell forward, his head made a terrible banging sound on the metal desk. David knew that in his whole life he would never get that sound out of his mind.

Aaron Kominski walked over to the businessman and felt his pulse. He looked at David and shook his head.

"How did you figure out that Willie was involved?"

In the police station, David was relaxing at his desk. During the day shift, Hank Hatfield used the same desk, so David was looking at pictures of his cute, red-headed kids. A couple of desks away, Gary was laboring at the computer station.

"I went to the Junction to talk to Hester Fernshaw about the night of the funeral reception. She told me that they had closed the restaurant early. At that time I suspected that Ceci or Rosie had stolen the key. I didn't think that they had killed Dorothy, but I thought they might have gone from the house that night to search it. I especially suspected Ceci because of that crowd she hangs out with. Someone from that river levee group could have gone with her and when they saw that Berta was in the way, well, a lot of those guys wouldn't have stopped at attacking an old lady. I thought that through, but I just couldn't buy it."

David paused to drink some of the coffee which Helen brought to him. Like Gary, she was hanging on to his every word.

"I also thought that something wasn't quite right with Leland Johannson's behavior. He never seemed worried enough about the restaurant. He deliberately seemed to keep his distance from it. And then he posts bail for a cook whom he barely knows?

Why? Maybe to keep the police from pursuing other leads. But his alibi for the night of the murder checked out. He was in his plane heading for Midland. And fortunately for him he had an alibi for the night of Berta's attack. Still I couldn't help thinking that he could have a motive, something that didn't have anything to do with the lottery ticket. And if he wanted to do something, it would be his style to hire someone else to do his dirty work."

"I knew he was very high on your list of possibilities when we got those telephone records," said Gary, "and found one number that was called a bit too much. But what made you think of that?"

"I heard some gossip about Opal Garfield and Willie Fernshaw. Opal told a friend that Willie Fernshaw had been at a drag race and had tried to pick her up. He was trying to impress her and bragged that he was in town to do some work for a very important man. Soon he would have plenty of money he told her. Opal turned him down of course. Told him that she never dated married men or wife beaters."

From her station, Helen made a snorting sound. David ignored it, because he knew some of the older women, like Helen Sinclair and Edna Grunderson, thought Opal was something of a tart. Like Shea, he knew that the sexy beautician might be a free spirit, but she was also a class act and too good for the likes of Willie Fernshaw.

"That's why I staked out the telephone box that night. If he was working for an important man, there were only a few people in town who would have need of such services. I had a hunch that the pay telephone number on Leland's records were being made to Willie. And my hunch turned out to be right."

"But how did you figure out it was an insurance scam?" asked Helen.

David shrugged. "Another lucky hunch. If it wasn't the lottery ticket, then the motive had to be something else. With a man like Leland Johannson involved, it had to be about money. What better way to bring in some quick cash than to collect on an insurance policy?"

He didn't mention that Shea had received the same intuition at the exact time or that she was his source for the gossip. She had asked him to keep her name out of any investigation, and David liked it best that way. He didn't like the thought of anyone going after Shea for passing along information to the police. Of course, Beau knew, and it was necessary to tell Aaron. David knew, however, that both men would be discreet.

"Every time I heard Bach or Albinoni or Thomas Tallis, it kept reminding me of something. But I just couldn't quite remember what it was," she had told him earlier. "Then when I was watching that television program about an insurance scam, it came to me. On the day of the Visitation at the funeral parlor, Bob Crockett had been talking about the fact that Leland Johannson wasn't paying insurance premiums for his employees. Marlene had said that he couldn't afford it. But I seemed to remember my grandmother telling me sometime ago that he always carried a lot of insurance on all his businesses. She knew, because she had seen the books. And everyone knew that he was having money problems. So when I saw that program, I thought that maybe he would try something like this."

David was impressed that Shea, with so much on her mind, had figured out the crime before anyone else.

"Isn't it funny," said Helen, "that the lottery ticket turned out to be worthless. And here y'all were thinking it was the reason for the murder."

David smiled. Since Helen was one of the town's most gifted gossips, the story was obviously all over the place. And if Helen bought it, so would everyone else.

"Thank goodness Shea inherited those investment bonds," sighed Helen. "At least she'll have something to fall back on."

When she returned home from the fire, Shea fell into bed exhausted.

"It's that young man again," said Mary, bustling into her bedroom with a tray, filled with pastries and hot coffee. "I told him you needed to get a wee bit of sleep, but he's been calling every hour."

Mary handed her the telephone and left the room.

"David," said Shea as she bit into a sopaipilla. "What happened?"

"I think you have pretty much figured it out," said David. "It was an insurance scam, and it was Leland Johannson."

"I just couldn't put together all the details. Fill me in," said Shea, taking another bite of a delicious apricot empanada. She was ravenous.

For the next few minutes, David retold the chronology of events, from the night her grandmother was murdered to last night's tragic ending.

"And what will happen to Willie now? He's facing a murder charge, isn't he?" asked Shea.

"Yes. And it will be life imprisonment at best. He's trying to make a deal with the district attorney right now. Good luck. The district attorney's not a forgiving type of guy."

Shea didn't want to think about that. He was the man who had killed her grandmother. It was hard to have any sympathy for his fate.

"So what I can't figure out, is why Marlene left town? It made both her and Bob look guilty."

"Well, you can ask them yourself. Bob called the Chief last night to say he was picking her up at the El Paso Airport early late last night. They should be arriving in town right about now. Marlene wants to talk to you."

"I'm on my way."

Dressing quickly in the same jeans and shirt from the night before, she caught up with Mary in the kitchen.

"Can you watch the baby again?" she asked. "I just checked him, and he's asleep."

"Of course. They'll be wanting you downtown."

Shea hopped into the Mustang for the short trip to the station.

Funny, she thought. When I got this loaner, I thought I would be running errands, not taking part in a murder investigation.

At the station house, she saw Gary Armstrong, Jaime Chavez, and David De Vargas standing in a huddle.

"They're inside with the Chief," David told her and led her into the office.

Shea saw Marlene and Bob sitting in vinyl-covered chairs in front of Beau's desk. Bob was holding Marlene's hand while she dabbed at her eyes with a handkerchief. The gesture reminded Shea of the Reading of the Will when she had done the same.

"Shea, I'm sorry. I'm so sorry. I didn't mean to hurt you," she said when the younger woman entered the room.

Bewildered, Shea looked at her without comprehension. "Marlene, I don't understand. Didn't they tell you that it was Leland Johannson and Willie Fernshaw who did all this?"

"Let me explain," interrupted Bob. "The night that Dorothy was killed, she told Marlene that she thought she had the winning lottery ticket worth millions. She told her not to tell anyone. Well, asking Marlene to keep a secret is like asking a chicken not to lay eggs. So Marlene done told Rosie who took her home that night. Then she called me. Course we were all plumb excited. Then Dorothy turns up dead. And ever body starts to suspect ever body else. Specially Marlene. She thought I had done it."

"I didn't want to think that, Bob," said Marlene. "But you did

157

have that assault on your record. And you did need money. So I kept going to Dorothy's house looking for that ticket. That's why I was going through her clothes. I thought if I could find the damn thing, that it would clear you."

"What were you going to do if you did find it?" asked Beau coldly.

"I was going to give it to Shea. I swear. Well, maybe not," Marlene finished lamely. "But I swear, Shea, I would have made sure you were taken care of."

"So what happened the night of the funeral reception? Neither of you stole the key," said David.

"We went to Hudson's Tavern for a few drinks. Then I told Marlene, let's just get out of town for a few days. You got some time off comin' and so do I. So we just took off. But on the way, Marlene, who had been tossin' back them beers, began to accuse me of killing Dorothy. I told her she was crazy to think that. She said she didn't want to be with me. I said that was just fine, and I let her off at a rest stop on the Interstate, just like I told you before."

"I was going to call Rosie for a ride, and I had actually dial the number," said Marlene. "But a trucker came by and offered me a lift to El Paso. I knew him real well, he was always coming by the Roadhouse. So I went to El Paso. And when I got there, I just kept going. I took a flight to Las Vegas."

"She did what she always does whenever life gets to be too much for her," said Bob. "She went gambling in them casinos. It's a curse, that's what it is. She's got a problem and don't she know it now."

"What are you going to do now?" asked Shea who felt betrayed once again. Although this was the second person who would have stolen from her given the chance, she could not be angry with Marlene. She felt too sorry for someone who had such an obsessive addiction.

"I had so many debts, and I just didn't know what to do . . ." Marlene couldn't finished the sentence, because by now she was crying too hard.

"So I'm sellin' my cabin and my motorboat to pay off them debts," finished Bob. "I know she's got a problem, but we can work it out together. We're going to move to Dallas where I hear they got some real good programs for gamblin' addicts."

Through her tears, Marlene tried to smile at Shea. "Honey, I'm real sorry for all the trouble. And I'm especially sorry that the ticket wasn't worth nothing."

"Are there going to be any charges against them?" Shea asked

David as they left the office.

"They're not really guilty of anything except mistrusting each other."

"That's good. What about Rosie and Ceci?"

"Why don't you ask them? They called here, and they both want to see you. I'll go with you."

They left in the Mustang for the short drive to the De Anda household. When they arrived, a wan-looking Ceci answered the door. She invited them into a house that smelled like death.

"The doctors say that our mother doesn't have much longer," said Rosie as they went into the living room. "The chemotherapy and drugs haven't worked, and the cancer is inoperable. It's really only a matter of days."

"I'm really sorry," said Shea sincerely.

"I'm sorry too," said Ceci. "I'm so sorry I took the key. And then that bastard Willie Fernshaw stole it from my purse. He heard me talking about it with Rosie. Don't blame Rosie. She didn't know what I had done, and she was trying to get me to give it back. It's just that for a few minutes while I was in your home, I thought I could do it. I thought if I could just find that lottery ticket, I could cash it in. Marlene wouldn't say anything if I gave her some money. And Bob wouldn't say anything if Marlene told him to keep quiet."

For a moment, the teenager couldn't continue. David and Shea waited patiently while she collected herself. Rosie couldn't seem to look at either of them. Her eyes seemed glued to the cabbage rose pattern in the faded carpet.

"It's been so hard these past few years for Rosie and me. All we seem to do is work and take care of our mother. It's like we were never going to have a life. I know that's no excuse, but it's how I felt," Ceci said weakly.

Shea could actually empathize with that.

"I wanted so much to get Ceci out of here," said Rosie, raising her eyes from the carpet. "She was beginning to hang out with the wrong crowd. So when I heard about the vandalism at your house and the attack on Berta, I thought that some of her friends might have done it. I knew she had taken the key. But I just couldn't turn her in."

"What are you going to do now?" asked David.

"I'm going to enter Mesa State University. I don't know what I want to do, maybe nursing or accounting. And Ceci thinks she wants to be a teacher. It all depends on whether or not we're in trouble."

She looked from Shea to David and then down at the carpet again.

"It's up to Shea if she wants to press charges," said David. "All Ceci did was to steal a key. She didn't do anything with it."

Shea shook her head. "I don't want to do anything like that. I know it wasn't right, but it won't help to start punishing people. I really do wish you both the best."

What she didn't say was that she really admired Rosie. Only two years older than her younger sister, she often seemed years older than Shea. She had so much on her shoulders. And there was really nothing wrong with Ceci except that she hadn't much adult guidance during her life. According to David, their father had left them ten years ago, and their mother had been sick for the past six years. The girls had practically been raising themselves. Shea felt they really deserved a break.

"I hope things get better for you," she told Rosie who walked them to the door. The young woman didn't answer. Shea thought she had never seen such sadness in one person's eyes in her whole life.

Two weeks later, Shea was sitting on the veranda on the porch swing. Life had returned to a much more normal routine. For one thing, Berta had returned from Mexico where she had left her elderly mother with her brother's family. She was now coming to the house at least three times a week to cook and clean to her heart's content. Shea even convinced her that she could give her a little extra to send to her brother for her mother's care. She had raised Berta's wages enough that she didn't need to work for anyone else unless she wished to do so.

From the beginning, Mary and Berta hit it off, primarily because Mary had the good sense to treat Berta as if she were the boss. At first Berta, five years Mary's senior, was somewhat suspicious that the newcomer would usurp her place, but once she was convinced that Mary would allow Berta to run the household whenever she was around, she decided that the nurse's aide was a very wise woman. Of course Berta and George continued to bicker, which pleased both of them no end.

Mark was doing much better, and Vanessa had assured Shea that he should be off the oxygen in another month's time. In the meantime Shea had contacted Father Jim about the Christianing ceremony. Shea, George, and Berta had attended the required classes, and the baptism would take place on the next Sunday. Already Shea had planned another reception, but this one would be much more joyous. Vases of roses from Alana's Flower and Gift Shop, a huge, frothy cake from Alberto's Bakery, and the most expensive Christianing gown available from Edna's Boutique had already been ordered.

Shea had even considered doing some remodeling on the house, but she decided she would wait awhile. Eventually, she promised herself, she would have to hire a contractor, because they really did need an extra bathroom at the very least. In the meantime she and George had cleared out the attack, and George was building bookshelves so she could go on a real book-buying spree. David had helped George move the computer furniture and equipment to the attic, and Shea had already begun to revise her dissertation. In a few months, she would think of sending it off to a publisher.

The extra room now became a guest room. She had hope that Shannon, her nine-year-old niece, would agree to spend some vacation time with her. It would seem like history repeating herself, she thought with more than a little nostalgia. Summertime should be spent swimming at the city recreation pool, afternoons at the Globe Theatre, evenings at the amateur rodeo competitions, and any spare time devouring novels. It shouldn't be spent in mourning or solving crimes, she told herself firmly. Never again.

Her thoughts, thankfully on more mundane subjects than murder, were interrupted when David De Vargas drove up in his jeep. He parked behind the larger cobalt blue Jeep Cherokee which now graced Shea's curved driveway. As he walked up the steps, he admired the young woman wearing a white tee-shirt with red lettering, white shorts,a nd a red baseball cap.

"So where's the sexy Mustang?" he asked.

"I really wanted to keep it," Shea groaned. " But right now the whole town thinks I didn't win a huge lottery. Buying a new car is one thing, but buying two cars would make everyone suspicious. So this is best."

"Yep, I think you're right," said David. "So did you hear that Rosie and Ceci De Anada both suddenly received four-year scholarships to Mesa State University?"

"Really?" asked Shea. "That's great news."

"Yeah," said David with a sidelong glance at her. "From an anonymous scholarship source. I just wonder if that was the same anonymous source who paid for their mother's funeral. Real convenient, wouldn't you say."

"I wouldn't know anything about that," said Shea, realizing that she sounded awfully prissy. "Have you heard anything about Hester Fernshaw?"

"Hester and Curtis decided to return to Michigan where they have family. It was just too much to deal with things around here. Although nobody blamed her. She and Curtis were victims of Willie Fernshaw as much as anybody else."

"That's right. I hope they'll be okay. Oh, I heard from Bob. He called a few days ago. Apparently he and Marlene are living in Dallas. They're both working at a nice restaurant , and she's attending counseling sessions at Gambler's Anonymous."

"I hope it works out for them. There is one more thing that I have to tell you," said David a little reluctantly.

"What is it?"

"Well, it seems that Willie Fernshaw got into a fight with another inmate while he was sitting in the county jail. He was killed."

Shea didn't know what to say. She was torn between feelings for her grandmother and sympathy for his family.

"At least this means there won't be a trial," continued David. "He had already confessed, and so the book is closed."

"I am relieved about that. So who's going to run Johannson's Market and Johannson's Feed and Grain now?"

"It seems that everything will revert to ownership by Olga Svenson, Leland's first wife. Apparently in their divorce settlement, the agreement was that Olga retained half-ownership of all the businesses, and if anything happened to either of them, the other one inherited everything."

"So we'll have the Svenson family returning to Mesa."

"Yes," agreed David. "She regained her maiden name after the divorce. After all, it was a name to be proud of. Her ancestors helped settle this town, just as yours did."

They sat in silent contemplation for a moment, enjoying the coolness of the morning.

"Well, are you ready to go?" asked David. He was wearing the same white tee shirt with red lettering, jeans and red cap.

"You bet. We're going to whip those Cardinals into shape so they can beat the Astros at the first softball game. If Gary Armstrong and Vanessa MacKenzie think they can outcoach us, they've got another think coming. This team will be tough, single-minded, and unstoppable."

"Shea," said David. "They're eight-year-olds."

"You can never start too soon to prepare for the Olympics. Imagine - a gold medal for the team from Mesa, Texas."

"Good Lord," mumbled David as they climbed into his jeep. "I've created a monster."

Mary O'Malley's Sopaipillas

2 cups flour

1 ½ t baking powder

1 t salt

1 cup cinnamon/sugar mixture

½ stick butter or margarine

¼ cup vegetable oil

1 cup milk

powder sugar

1. Cream butter and flour, baking soda, and salt.
2. Gradually add milk. Knead the mixture and roll it out on a floured surface.
3. Cut into 8 pieces.
4. Fry in hot oil until lightly browned.
5. Shake cinnamon and sugar mixture over patties.
6. Sprinkle with powder sugar.

*La Mesa Noticia,*Sunday, June 30

(Editor's Note: The personal ad from June 15 should have read "my *truck* is missing again.")